Champion in the Darkness

Tyrean Martinson

Dear Staub Family,
May your faith always be strong and the Lord guide you in all.
-Tyrean Martinson

Published by Tyrean Martinson with Wings of Light Publishing

ISBN-13:
978-1481982740

ISBN-10:
1481982745

This book is available at most online retailers.

Cover Art by Stephanie Glover

DEDICATION

This book is dedicated to my mom and dad, my Grandma Pearl, my husband, my daughters, and most of all to Jesus, the light of the world.

CONTENTS

Contents

"In him was life, and that life was the light of men. The light shines in the darkness, but the darkness has not understood it." John 1:4-5

1 VISIONS

Lightning struck from the thick black clouds all around her. The burning man raised a fiery sword above his head and Clara cowered in the wet, slimy mud with a broken sword in her hands. Sharp, harsh sounds of fighting surrounded her, and the smell of smoke filled her lungs. When the dark lightning flashed again and the fiery sword began its descent, Clara's eyes flew open and she gasped for air.

The recurring nightmare had struck again. The lightning burned into the blackness of sleep was replaced by sunlight pouring into her room, hitting her directly in the face. She closed her eyes, and tried to remember the details. She felt like she had to replay it, had to understand it. The darkness had been filled with the noise of battle, but underneath that, there had been chanting voices. It didn't make sense.

Despite being covered in sweat from her nightmare, she shivered and goose bumps rose on her arms. Burrowing into her quilts, she curled into a ball on her side.

"Wake up, sleepyhead," sang out her father's baritone voice. "Rise and shine and give God the glory, glory."

Clara smiled under the covers, but groaned out loud. At fifteen, she didn't really want her dad singing songs to her in the morning, did she? Well, maybe a little, and his job as a Shepherd and teacher just seemed to pour out over in all aspects of his life. Shepherds led their flocks in prayer, study, and song, and her Dad's special love was music.

Clara opened her eyes and pulled the covers back just enough to see her Dad. His eyes twinkled. He had always been the morning person in the family, waking well before sunrise to start his prayers of thanksgiving and his study of the sacred scrolls.

"Am I raising a sword master, or a butterfly?" he asked, teasingly. "You keep wrapping yourself in a cocoon each night, so one of these mornings, I'll expect you to have wings."

"Dad," she groaned again, and frowned at him, "I'm not a little girl anymore. I know I'm not going to grow wings overnight."

His face stilled for a moment, looking almost sad. "Ah, but you have," he said. "You've grown up, and today your wings will take the form of a sword of power, the weapon of masters and senior apprentices."

He sat on the edge of her bed, and cupped her face in his soft hands. "You'll always be my little girl, even when you're off fighting and I won't be able to protect you." He leaned down and kissed her forehead. "May the Lord lift you up on wings like eagles, and keep you safe."

Clara wished her dad wouldn't be so melodramatic about her growing up, but she knew he meant well. If he hadn't been so serious already, she might have told him about the nightmares. As it was, she didn't want to concern him any further. She reached up and hugged him hard, squeezing him to let him know she wasn't going anywhere yet.

He held her against his lean frame for a few minutes, and then let her go. Standing up quickly, he brought a hand to his eyes, turning away from her. His voice came out husky, when he spoke. "Time for breakfast. Mom toasted some nut bread, and cut some papaya just for you."

"Thanks Dad," Clara said, trying to put reassurance in her voice. After he left, she changed quickly from her pajamas into loose fitting pants and a shirt. Both were gray, marking Clara as a sword apprentice. She stood in front of her small mirror to braid her shoulder length reddish blonde hair, and tried to frown at her reflection. It didn't work. The freckles across her upturned nose seemed to refuse to be serious for long. She wondered how many sword masters had freckles. It didn't seem fair, even if she did like a good prank now and then. Her lifelong passions included sword work, and studying the legends of sword masters. She couldn't imagine any of the Champions or heroes of the Triune Halls in ages past with freckles and an upturned nose. The pictures in the history texts made the Champions and heroes appear somber and determined.

Clara crept out of her room on her tiptoes, hoping to catch her mom unawares. They often tried to sneak up on each other, practicing sword scout skills with a bit of play. As she paused outside the threshold of the kitchen, she peered in carefully at her mother.

In their small kitchen, her mother was dressed in sword master black with the insignia of the Sword Guards on each shoulder. Her mom's straight blonde hair was pulled back in a tight braided bun, and she stood facing the window.

"Juice or tea for breakfast, Clara?" her mother asked, not turning from her work at the cutting board.

"Tea would be wonderful, mom," Clara said, slightly envious of the way her mother seemed to sense her presence even when she had been sure that she had been silent.

"Good, then why don't you get that, while I finish cutting the fruit," her mother said.

Clara found the tea and the tea pot, and quickly filled the earthenware pot with the hot water already steaming on their stovetop. Setting the tea pot on the small round table, Clara drew out three cups and placed them in their usual places. The small round table where they ate most of their meals only fitted up to four people, and Clara liked the coziness of it. She sat on the side that faced the open living area, her dad faced the open window, and her mom sat nearest the stove, always ready to jump up and stir something, if needed.

Everything felt so normal this morning, as her mother brought the fruit to the table, and her father reached out his hands to pray.

The words of the prayer tumbled over her head, in a comforting cadence, but Clara was thinking about the day ahead of her, and tingling with excitement. She started bouncing her legs under the table.

"And please give Clara wisdom today in the Chamber of Choice, Lord. Amen." Her father finished praying and winked at her.

Clara stopped bouncing her legs, and winked back at him.

"You're ready for today, Clara," said her mother, covering one of Clara's hands with her calloused right hand. "I'm proud of you, and will always be."

"Thanks Mom," Clara said, smiling widely.

"Now, get some food into you, so you can keep your strength up," her mother said, pulling back her hand and picking up a thick slice of nut bread.

Clara did the same, thankful for the delicious food that warmed her and relaxed her. Her mom and dad shared a lot of duties around their small apartment home, in keeping with their busy schedules as Sword Guard and Shepherd Teacher. Clara helped them by keeping her own things picked up and clean, along with helping with the roof garden during the summer months.

After their breakfast, Clara went back to her room and put on all of her practice armor. A sword belt, boots, hard leather breastplate, wrist guards, a close fitting helmet, and a small pack with essential supplies all went on easily as they had every morning for the last seven years.

When she went to sheathe her sword, she paused for a moment, looking at her distorted reflection in its surface. Today she would replace her training blade with a sword of power, the weapon of Triune Hall Sword Masters. She would almost miss the training sword. It fit so well in her hand. She sheathed that blade one last time, and strapped her small round shield to her pack.

Back in the kitchen, her mother and father were washing up the breakfast dishes together in companionable silence, affectionately bumping into one another as they worked.

"I'm ready to go," Clara said.

They turned, her mother wiping her hands on the dish towel that her father held for drying. Her mother's blue eyes crinkled at the corners, and she smiled slightly. "You look like a young master already," she said. Then she crossed the small room in a few steps and folded Clara in her arms. "You'll always be my baby, but I'm so glad you've chosen the way of the sword, Clara. You can take care of yourself and your friends, and I don't have to fear for you."

Clara's dad laughed a short laugh. "Our baby's putting herself in the path of sharp edges, but you are less worried for her than if she chose a Shepherd's robe? You still amaze me, dearest."

Clara's mom squeezed Clara one more time, and then turned to her husband, her back slightly tense. "You know why, Farrald," she said quietly.

As always, Clara wanted to ask just what her mother meant by that remark, so like many other remarks made around their home that remained unexplained. Her mother had promised to tell her more about her past when Clara was old enough. She hoped that today might become that day, or after her inclusion in the circle of Sword Masters.

Farrald wrapped his arm around Juliay, and kissed the top of her head. He smiled at Clara. "You're going to be late if you dawdle with us, Clara." He came over and gave her a short hug, and then stepped back. "We'll see you at luncheon today, to celebrate."

"See you then," Clara said, and still smiling she left their apartment, going down the outdoor steps past the music store below them.

The instruments hung silent at this hour since customers normally appeared just a few hours before luncheon and left a while after dinner. Clara glanced over the instruments as she passed, wondering which one she would play if she could. Her dad played the lute and the pipes. She enjoyed the music of the thrimble, a three stringed instrument with a thick neck and a short body. Then she put her hand on the leather wrapped hilt of her sword, the instrument she had chosen years ago as a child in the Desert district.

Clara followed the shortest route to the Triune Halls, hardly noticing anything around her, thinking over all the choices she had made that led to today's choice, the entrance into the Crystal Sword chamber. As long as she could remember, she had tried sword fighting with sticks. When Master Stelia had come to the Triune Halls of the Desert district, Clara had wanted to follow the mysterious, foreign swordswoman everywhere she went. When the Triune Council decided they needed her parents' skills in Skycliff, the capital city of Septily, she had told them formally that she wished to enter training as a Sword Master. At eight, she had been the second youngest apprentice. Her friend, Salene, had been the next youngest. So many days of training had led to this day.

She wondered what kind of sword she would choose. She had thought about it many times before, but still didn't know.

She felt a swirl of excitement as she thought through all the colors of crystal swords available: yellows, browns, blues, purples, greens, reds, oranges, and even blacks. She knew each had meaning, and each matched the temperament and soul of the master that carried them. Her mother carried a dark navy sword with hints of purple in its depths, which stood for determination and nobility.

Suddenly, a hand blocked her vision, and she stopped, blinking, at her friend Salene. With a silly grin on her face, Salene didn't look like the daughter of an out of favor noble. Her short dark hair framed her narrow face, and she looked physically stronger than any of the noblewomen who fluttered around the dress shops. Her dark eyes twinkled with merriment.

"Are you sure you're ready for today with your head in the clouds?" Salene teased, waving her hand back and forth in front of Clara.

Clara batted her hand away, and stuck her tongue out at her friend. "I'm ready enough," she said. "The Sword Council grilled me for an hour yesterday, even after the Sword Teacher's board examined me."

"I know," Salene said softly. She put her arm through Clara's and tugged her down the street. "But you're ready, so let's get you there, and get it done, even if that means I'll be missing you after that."

"I won't be leaving for my practical internship for at least six months," Clara said, then she waved at Mr. Balent, their friendly neighborhood baker.

He waved and threw them both warm rolls that they caught easily. Clara started munching hers right away, but Salene tucked hers into her satchel.

"Yes, but you'll be busy with your duties," said Salene, echoing Clara's dad's worries. "And when you go, you have to visit each of the seven halls from the seven districts of Septily," she said. "That's going to take a while, and I'm going to miss beating you at footraces."

"Miss beating me, or getting beaten?" Clara asked, jostling Salene to the side of the street.

Salene disentangled herself from Clara's arm, gave her a playful shove back, and said, "Beat me to the Hall gate, then, Master Swordswoman." She took off at a sprint down the street.

Clara dug her toes into the hard cobblestones beneath her, and ran after her friend, throwing everything she had into the moment.

Ahead of her, Salene navigated her way between early morning vendors who were attempting to set up their sales wagons on the street sides.

Clara scrambled after her, barely missing a bird seller, and forced to jump over a basket of eggs. Angry shouts followed her, but she kept running hard.

Salene took a right turn early, and they sprinted down an open alleyway and onto the Palace Way. This early, there were no courtiers about, only two of the King's mysterious Shadow Guards at the gate. Salene and Clara looked at each other, and pushed themselves harder.

At the intersection of Palace Way, and Hall Road, Clara stretched past Salene, managing to stay a hand ahead of her until they reached the cherry tree at the outer walk. Breathless, she slowed her pace and grinned at Salene.

Salene threw up her hands, and said, "All right, in footraces you beat me half the time."

"Only half?" Clara teased, smiling, and then she went quiet.

As they entered the gate to the Triune Hall, Clara always felt honored to simply be there. Today she felt even more awed than usual. She had been training for today her whole life. She felt as if time slowed around her, as she took in the scene around her.

Each stone of the Three Halls was carved with words and decorations, and each was kept clean by apprentices like Clara herself. The courtyard was paved with multi-colored slabs of stone, and there were three oases of gardens in the midst of it with grassy areas to sit, and trees to climb or pick fruit from depending on the season. The open blue sky above them, the scents of the blossoms, the sounds of the voices around them made Clara almost want to stop this moment in time forever. The anticipation and excitement building in her felt full and sweet in and of itself, and she tried to hold onto it.

She paused at the fountain in the courtyard and looked down into the shallow water which lapped gently against the marble sides. "I have been blessed."

Salene put her hand on Clara's shoulder and squeezed. "You've been dedicated to the way of the Sword for as long as I can remember. Remember when you greeted me with that stick and challenged me to a bout?"

Clara smiled ruefully. She had been a terror of the Desert Halls when she was growing up. "I don't think I'll ever forget that."

"Well, time to make a new memory," Salene encouraged her. She stepped away from the fountain and led the way into the vast entry hall.

Following her, Clara gazed up at the marble floor and tall columns, a far cry from the smaller and simpler Triune Hall structure in the Desert district. It made sense that the capital of Septily would have the most beautiful and largest of the Triune Halls, outfitted with a glorious cathedral, and special training areas for each of the three disciplines: The Sword, the Truth, and the Way, or better known as: The Sword Masters, the Law-Givers and The Shepherds, all bound together by their belief in one faith.

Clara knew that not everyone in Septily believed in the Lord, the Creator, Savior, and Spirit, but she couldn't imagine not believing. To believe in nothing made no sense to her, and to believe in a stone god made last year in a rock quarry didn't make sense to her either.

Salene broke into her thoughts with a squeeze on her arm. "Hey, you're ready, you know that, right?"

"I think so," said Clara, realizing that she was nervous as well as excited.

"Then I'll see you at luncheon," Salene said, and she walked away, leaving Clara at the reception desk that stood between the Sword Master's Council Chamber and the Chamber of Choice.

Clara approached the reception desk, where a young sword guard she didn't recognize sat waiting.

"May I help you, apprentice?" he asked, in a voice thick with burr of the Forester province.

"Yes, thank you," Clara said. "I'm to meet Master Dantor here, and enter the Chamber of the Sword this morning."

He smiled at her, and then looked down at his papers. "You're expected," he said. "Although you're younger than I thought you would be."

Clara merely nodded, knowing that she was younger than most students who entered their mastership. At fifteen, she had already passed up students two to three years older than herself.

"You're to wait there, by the doors to the Chamber," said the sword guard.

"Thank you, sir," said Clara. She walked slowly over the doors, which were carved with several scenes, the history of the Champions of Septily. The first Champion, Champion Elar, overlapped the two doors at the center. Champion Elar had fought back the divisive forces of the Dark Sisterhood and brought seven kingdoms together to form Septily itself. The carving showed him standing in the midst of a map of Septily, fighting back a dark cloud over his head. She shivered at the sight of that cloud now, reminded of her nightmare.

Champion Elar had been called by the Lord to serve with King Wilstorm nearly two thousand years ago. Since then, four other Champions had been called to serve the country. Depictions of Champion Ferris, Champion Tamara, Champion Hest, and Champion Samuel ringed the one of Champion Elar. More space had been left on the doors for future carvings of future Champions.

From Clara's understanding there were Champions that showed up in other countries all over the world of Aramatir, and Clara had studied some of the legends about them as part of her training. Each Champion held a special place of honor in the Triune Halls, chosen by the Lord of all to be a light in the darkest times. The Triune Halls were an over-reaching form of government that transcended country boundaries, and knit the fabric of Aramatir together. The Champions upheld the highest values of faith, strength, loyalty, honor, and sacrifice.

Clara had tried to lose herself in the history of the Champions, but she felt the swell of anticipation in every moment. She had tried to focus on the details of the carving in front of her, but as time passed, she became more aware of her fast pulse and the lightness in her chest.

Finally, Master Dantor exited the Sword Council door to her left, and crossed the room towards her. His stern, lean face was furrowed in thought.

She saluted him, with her hand to her heart, and he returned the salute somberly.

He stood in front of her and observed her for a moment, then ran his hand over his short, dark hair and sighed.

Instantly cold sweat broke out on Clara's arms. Something had to be very wrong. Master Dantor didn't sigh without reason. She couldn't imagine what it could be. Her mind raced through everything that had happened during all the tests she had endured to reach the Mastery level of training. "Sir?" she said, not really knowing what to ask.

He took a deep breath and let it out slowly, and then nodded to himself. "Clara, do you know the legends of the Champions?"

Clara looked at the doors in front of her, as if they held the answers she needed to pass this final, and unexpected test. "I know them, Master Dantor."

Master Dantor followed her gaze, and smiled briefly. "I hope you know them beyond the depictions on those doors after all these years, Clara."

"Yes, sir," Clara said, feeling a little irritated now. Hadn't this been covered in the grilling interview she had completed just yesterday in the Sword Council chambers?

Master Dantor's dark eyes seemed to bore down on her, but Clara kept her poise and waited.

Dantor looked over at the doors again. "Some of the Shepherds are granted with visions from the Lord regarding the future of our land and the future of the Halls. Some have even seen glimpses of the next Champion."

Clara wanted to ask why this mattered to her, but she kept her silence. She knew that Dantor wasn't finished yet. He seemed as if he were leading to something.

"It is rare, but sometimes others receive visions of that kind. Many years ago, I had a vision of the next Champion. In my vision she was battle-stained and weary, although young in years. I had the vision confirmed by one of the Shepherds from the Hall of Wisdom, and as the years went by, I searched for her but never found her." He looked at her directly now, his eyes like coals against his tan, weather-beaten face. "Last night I had the same vision, and the Champion had your face."

2 STRUCK BY DESTINY

Master Dantor's words washed over Clara like a huge wave, and she merely stood there. She felt as if she had been covered in a deluge, and yet as if something in her wanted to burst forth and claim everything he said, as if her soul was swelling inside her chest. Her palms began to sweat, and she felt as if the room expanded and contracted around her. "The next Champion," she said quietly. "I'm . . .the next . . .Champion?" She swayed slightly, and then stepped forward to place her hand on the carvings on the door in front of her. The wood felt soothing under her skin. The figures blurred, and she realized that tears were in her eyes. "I'm only an apprentice," she whispered.

"You are the best apprentice I've ever trained, Clara," said Master Dantor.

Clara turned to look at him, checking to see if he was in earnest.

He smiled and nodded. "You know I don't give praise lightly, so don't ask to hear that again."

"Thank you, Master Dantor." She had the sudden urge to hug him, but didn't dare. His usual gruffness didn't invite those kinds of actions by his students. So she merely said, "You have been a good teacher."

"Don't think your lessons are over, Clara, just because you're a Master apprentice and have a destiny," he said. "You've got work to do, if you're going to give glory to the Lord as a Champion, a lot of work in tactics, if I'm not mistaken, plus your internship . . .although," he frowned, "I think your internship is going to be rather unpleasant and all too real."

"What do you mean?" asked Clara, surprised.

"As I said, in my vision you were battle-stained and weary before you received your Crystal Sword . . .and you won't receive it in there," he said, pointing to the doors.

Clara felt a stab of disappointment at that. She had longed to enter the Chamber of the Sword for so many years that being denied felt like a wound, but that wound was dulled by Dantor's prophecy, and knowing, somehow, that he was right. She would be Champion. She wasn't ready. She wasn't sure how it was possible, but somehow she knew deep inside her that it was true.

She trailed her fingers over the carving of Champion Elar for a moment, noticing for the first time the determined set of his face. Pulling herself away from the doors, she faced Master Dantor, putting her hand over her heart and saluting him. "What are the next steps in my training, Master Teacher?"

He smiled. "This morning I will be in a special session with the Sword Council, and you are free. At luncheon, I expect to reveal all this to your parents. Then, this afternoon, you will be tutored by Master Stelia. Consider today a partial holiday, apprentice. For after this, you will be working harder than ever before." He looked as if he were about to say more, and then stopped himself, pursing his lips.

Clara wasn't ready to hear anything more about his vision yet. She had too much to take in already.

"Thank you, sir," she said, and then turned to leave. She realized that she wasn't sure what she should do with this free time. If she were Salene, she would probably run to the library and research the previous Champions, getting beyond the surface of the history they had in their classes. But she wasn't Salene, and she needed space to think. She knew exactly where she needed to go.

Braced against the crumbling brown ramparts of Skycliff's seawall,

Clara leaned into the misty blue horizon. Ships with billowing sails headed into the distance. Closer to the cliffs the gulls swooped and cried. Clara watched the cup of their white wings, and raised her arms, mimicking their movement. Letting the sea air fluff her wide sleeves like wings, she closed her eyes for a moment and imagined that would-be Champions could even fly.

The dream from this morning came back to her, and this time she saw a flash of gold and white wings, a broken young man, and then darkness. She dropped her arms and opened her eyes, trying to get brightness above her dispel her vision. Then she spread her arms again, and bowed her head slightly, like she had seen her father do so many times. Words failed her. She had to concentrate on the light of the Lord, the light she remembered from the day of her baptism. Slowly, she felt peace start to flow into her, relaxing her muscles with warmth. "Lord, I need you," she finally said.

Heavy tramping boot steps interrupted her quiet. Clara hastily snapped her arms down. The King's mercenary Shadows, hired to replace the King's lost faith in the Trinity Sword Guards, were patrolling the wall. She stepped over to one of the archer's alcoves in the wall, and backed into its dark recesses. She wouldn't be able to see them round the bend in the wall now, but she hoped they would also not see her.

They passed in a loud stamping of feet. Silent in voices, but not in manners, the Shadows frightened many in the capital. Clara didn't admit her fear to others, but she felt it. Something wasn't right about them in their dark red armor, and their black masks. They were unnerving, even when their eyes weren't on you. When they entered a quarter in the city, it became quiet. They seemed to spread fear with their silence and rough manners, taking what they wanted from the merchants, and looking menacingly on anyone who asked for payment. When the Sword Guards and the Sword Council had approached the King to discuss the matter, he had sent them away with no explanation and no reparation. The capital had become thick with the growing tension between the King and the Council.

She counted five groups of four men, one of their usual groups of twenty. However, they normally walked the wall clockwise from the palace around the city. Today they were walking counter-clockwise from the palace, heading towards the Triune Halls first, and not towards the market first. The direction bothered her, but she couldn't really put a reason on her feelings. It just seemed wrong that they would head towards the Triune Halls. She wondered, if she could stand and look across the city, if she would see another group marching in a different direction on the opposite wall.

When their footsteps were long gone, Clara heard another set of steps coming up the nearest stairwell that led into the city. These steps were light, like the pattering of rain. Salene's slim, familiar figure passed her hiding place.

Clara smiled to herself and eased her way out of the cubby. She closed the gap between herself and Salene, and then tapped her friend's shoulder.

Salene gave a satisfying jump, but turned with a knife in her right hand.

"Oh, you," she said, rolling her eyes. She sheathed her weapon.

Clara chuckled. "You should have seen the look on your face!"

"You know I hate it when people say that," Salene said. Then she looked pointedly at Clara's sword belt. "I heard you didn't get to enter the Chamber after all. Dantor sent a message to Master Jessup, and I was dismissed from classes to find you and offer you encouragement. So what happened?"

Clara bit her lip and looked out at the ocean. She hesitated to tell Salene about becoming the next Champion, because it seemed like some kind of crazy brag or prank. The truth would come out. She might as well be the one to tell it. "Master Dantor had a vision years ago, and then again last night. I'm supposed to be the next Champion of Septily. I'll get my sword in the middle of a battle and not now." She glanced at Salene, to see if her friend believed her and how she was taking it.

Salene's eyes widened and her mouth gaped, and then she shut it quickly. "You're joking with me, right? This is another one of your pranks?"

"It's not," Clara said. She swallowed and plunged ahead. "I had a strange dream last night, and then when I was standing here, I had a vision of that dream again. Well, not a vision, but images: a battle, voices changing in the darkness, a storm overhead."

"That doesn't sound good," Salene said. She looked out at the ocean too. I've always thought the Champions lived rough lives, and I wouldn't wish that on myself or anyone I cared about."

Surprised, Clara let out a short bark of laughter. "Thanks for making me feel so much better," she said sarcastically.

"You're welcome. That's what friends are for," said Salene, and then she smiled crookedly. "So, you're to be the Champion. I'm not sure Skycliff's ready for you."

"So, one last prank, one last time, before I have to get all serious about being a Champion?" Clara asked, winking at her friend.

Salene groaned, and pretended to slump her shoulders. "What now? Are we going to use my old noble heritage to sneak into the museum and borrow the first scepter of Septily, then try to pass it off as part of our history and tactics lessons?"

"No, no, nothing that simple," said Clara, smirking. "I think we should . ." she thought for a moment, and then came up with something she hoped Master Stelia would actually be proud of her for doing. "I think we should climb the castle walls, and spy on the Shadow Guards." She said it in a rush, and the gasped for breath. "And it's not really a prank. We would be gathering information for the Triune Halls."

Salene looked horrified, her head shaking as Clara spoke. "Clara, that's serious business. We could be imprisoned and executed for treason." She lowered her voice, and her eyes narrowed. "We are not spying on the Shadow Guards. King Alexandros may have lost faith in the Triune Halls, and the Sword Masters, but we should give him no reason to mistrust us. Time will prove our loyalty to him, as well as to the Lord."

Clara took a deep breath, feeling more committed to her scheme now. "The Triune Council needs to know more about the Shadow Guards, you know that."

Salene ran her hand across her face for a moment, and then said in an even tone. "That's a job for Master Scouts, and not apprentices."

"If you don't join me, I'll do it on my own," Clara said, and then she turned on her heel and started jogging down towards the palace.

"Clara," Salene hissed. She caught up to Clara easily and clamped her hand down on Clara's arm.

"Ow!" Clara tried to pull away from Salene's crushing grip, and stopped, wrestling with her.

After a few minutes, the matter was settled, at least for Clara. She held Salene in a tight grip, kneeling against the stones beneath them. "I'm going to spy on the King," she growled, "and you can't stop me."

"You can't go anywhere if you have to hold onto me the whole time," Salene stated calmly.

"Oh!" Clara released her in frustration, and threw her hands up in the air. "Fine. What shall I do on my last free day before the Council announces that I'm the next Champion of Septily, and I'm expected to be serious all the time?"

"Spar with me," said Salene. "Isn't that what we always do when we hit a snag in our plans? Take it to one of the weapons rings?"

"All right," Clara acquiesced, but inside she was planning a route to the castle that she could take later than night.

"I'm sure that not all Champions were serious all the time," said Salene. "It's just not stuff that gets written in the history scrolls, that's all."

3 SWORD COUNCIL

With her back to one wall, Stelia Southern waited patiently for the Sword Council meeting to begin. She leaned back in her wooden chair, and stretched out her long legs under the table in front of her.

The Sword Council met in a warm room, close to the center of the Triune Halls. The ceiling was of medium height, and the stone floor was unadorned. The tables were set in a square, with the head of the council, Master Theran, sitting at the center of the one closest to the door. She sat on his left, and Master Talz, a middle aged Sword Guard, sat two chairs away from his right. Master Talz also had his legs stretched out under the table, and he checked his weapons reflexively as he waited. Stelia caught herself mimicking his actions. It seemed a normal habit for every weapons master. Talz caught her eye and winked. She smiled back, but didn't wink. She didn't want to give the wrong impression. Only one man interested her in Skycliff, and he wasn't here yet.

Master Harthan, another Guard, sat at the table opposite to Master Theran with Master Bella, a Guard on his right and Master Nelson, an older teacher, on his left. They were involved in a quiet discussion, and were glancing occasionally at the map behind Master Theran.

Master Crall was around one corner, as far away from everyone as he could be as usual. His wispy white hair barely covered his head, and he appeared to be muttering angrily to himself, casting dark glances around the room. Stelia didn't know what was off about Master Crall, but she knew that something wasn't right about him. She knew he didn't like her, because of her background, but his treatment of the Sword Council as a whole seemed wrong. He was always on edge.

Finally, the door opened, and Stelia watched Dantor enter the council room. His graceful, powerful stride always caught her attention, and sent thrills through her. She knew the students thought of him only as a gruff taskmaster, but she saw a handsome, confidant man, hard on his students only because he felt he needed to be. Trying to get a read on the situation with Clara, she focused on his face. His eyes were bright with happiness and pride. His jaw was relaxed. So the meeting with Clara had gone well.

She smiled to herself. As the first person to welcome her without reservations into the Triune Halls, Clara had become dear to her. As the daughter of her friend, Juliay, she was twice as dear. Stelia wondered which type of sword she carried now, after her trial in the Chamber of Choice.

Master Theran, the head of the sword council, tapped the table with his hand. "Order, everyone."

Stelia sat forward in her chair. She felt her stomach tighten at the thought of what her information was going to bring to the table.

"Master Dantor, will you please begin with your report on apprentice Clara," Master Theran directed.

Dantor remained standing by his seat, and looked first at Theran, and then around the room, pausing briefly when he looked at Stelia.

Stelia felt her insides grow warm at his glance, and she looked down for a moment, fiddling with the end of her blonde braid.

"As many of you know, I had a vision years ago, of our next Champion. Last night, I had the same vision, and the Champion is Clara."

Stelia felt stunned, but didn't have time to react.

"Preposterous!" shouted Master Crall. She is already the youngest apprentice to be accepted for Mastership, and now you say she is to be Champion? This is merely a way for you to show off and to puff up an ambitious apprentice."

"Please listen, Crall," said Master Theran. "Dantor's vision has been confirmed by three Shepherds, and he is not the kind of Master who enjoys showing off for anyone's benefit."

"Prophecies and visions are an unproven method for decision making, Master Theran," Master Crall argued. "Septily hasn't seen a Champion since the year 1200 A.F., and we know that if such things as Champions existed one should have helped us in the Hundred Years Tri-Kingdom War. Making our decisions based on nonsense like -

"Silence, Crall," stated Master Theran heavily. "Your lack of historical knowledge is nearly as bad as your lack of faith. One more word about not believing in Champions, and I will have you removed from this Council permanently."

Crall continued to mumble angrily.

"You wish to leave now?" asked Master Theran.

"No," Crall said.

Stelia wondered why Crall hadn't been removed years ago, but sitting on the rotating seat for Sword Scouts, she held her opinions to herself.

"May we return to our order of business, Master Theran?" asked Master Talz in his firm, but quiet voice. He held himself erect now, no longer lounging, but paying close attention, as all the Masters were. A vision of a new Champion also meant the growing potential for problems, for Champions only arose in times of great need.

Stelia felt concern growing in her for Clara. The girl seemed too young, and too inexperienced for real battle. Stelia had been training longer, and fighting bloodier battles by the time she reached Clara's age, but Clara had led a privileged life of classroom tactics. She felt a sudden and keen new appreciation for Dantor's harsh training methods.

"Yes, please continue Master Dantor," said Master Theran. He turned slightly in his seat, to indicate that Dantor had his full and utmost attention.

"We know, from confirmed visions, that Clara will become our Champion in a time of battle, and we know that the Drinaii are at our Southern border. The King has refused a meeting with the Triune Council, and his mercenary friends, the Shadow Guards, have grown in number." Dantor ran his hand over his short, dark hair. "I wish we had a better understanding of the nature of the King's relationship with his mercenaries. If we could trust them, we could use them at the border."

Stelia leaned forward, and raised her hand slightly.

Master Theran waved his hand at her. "Master Stelia has news in regard to this matter that will reveal the motives of the Shadow Guard."

"Yes, Master Theran," Stelia said, standing up, and moving to the map. "We know their troops are here, between Desert Hold and Trent, and there by Gallowy. There are only two centuries of Drinaii at each border crossing." She took a deep breath and plunged into the unpleasant task of reminding them of who she was and where she came from. "As you know I served as a Drinaii once under the Dark Sisterhood, and I know intimately the way they arrange their attacks. They prefer subterfuge and trickery to open battles. I have long believed that the Drinaii might try to infiltrate our borders, and I have recently learned that I am right."

"Impossible!" shouted Crall. He stood as if to make a point.

"Please allow Master Stelia to finish her briefing," Master Theran growled.

"How do we know we can trust her? She is the adopted daughter of that witch, Kalidess, and you know it!" Crall pointed his finger accusingly at Master Theran.

Stelia felt herself pinned under the gazes of the entire Sword Council. She wished she could hide her shame, make her past disappear, but it wasn't possible. It marked every part of her, even her name.

Theran stood, and put his hand on Stelia's shoulder. "Master Stelia is no longer of the Dark Sisterhood, or the Drinaii. She left that past behind her, and has been absolved of all sin by our Lord, by the Triune Council, and by the laws of Septily. She has served us faithfully for many years now. You will listen to her report, and treat her with respect." He glared at Crall, and looked around the room at the other masters.

Thankfully, the other masters merely nodded, as if Theran's words were obvious.

"Hmmph," Crall grumbled. "I wish to take my leave of this council." He gathered his papers, and prepared to leave.

"You may leave under oath, and no other way," said Master Theran, walking to intercept Master Crall. "Draw your sword, and give your oath to the Lord, to this council, and the Triune Halls.

Master Crall tried to sidestep Master Theran, and Master Theran easily blocked him, grabbed him by the scruff of his collar, and yanked Master Crall's sword out of his scabbard.

Stelia sucked in her breath at the sight of Master Crall's sword. Without color or shine, it was as gray as stone.

The other Masters gasped audibly.

"It is as I have long suspected, Crall, you have lost your faith," said Master Theran. His voice became soft and sad, and his shoulders sagged. "How long has it been this way, my old friend?"

"As if you care!" Crall twisted in Master Theran's grasp, but was unable to break free.

"I do care," Master Theran said. "A sword of power does not go dull if the faith of the Master is strong. The longer it is dull, the harder it will be to regain it."

Crall shrugged, and then closed his eyes. "It's been seven years, since the Triune Council decided not to back King Alexandros' bid for vengeance. The Champion should have arrived then. Now, it's too late." He sank wearily towards the floor. Master Talz caught him, and quickly bound his hands in front of him.

"What do you mean?" Master Theran asked, standing above Crall with the dull stone sword in his hands.

"She'll tell you," said Crall, pointing at Stelia. "I don't understand why she hasn't been in the Chamber of Choice yet. You all obviously believe in her, and she obviously believes in the Lord. What's holding her back?"

"I am not worthy," said Stelia, feeling the weight of her old sins pressing down on her.

"We have offered, but she will not go in, until her debt is paid," said Master Theran. "Although I believe it has been paid twice over."

Master Harthan, who had been silent up to this point, tapped the table for attention, and then spoke. "I agree with you Master Theran, but I believe we should hear Master Stelia's report since it sounds as if it will bear on our current dilemma."

"We all know that King Alexandros has been distancing himself from the Triune Halls since the death of his wife. He wanted revenge on the Rrysorri, who he blamed for her murder, but the Triune Council, and the District Governors refused to support a war for vengeance, especially since no proof existed of Rryssori involvement. He disbanded his private Sword Guards last year, and replaced them with the Shadows. Their armor is similar to that of the Drinaii army, although newer in make so I have suspected them for this last year, but had been unable to confirm my suspicions until last night. I overheard two of them at the castle gate. They speak Drinaii."

"You're saying that the Drinaii are here and have already surrounded our King?" asked Master Harthan.

"I believe that the King may be in league with the Drinaii," she said simply.

"It's worse than that," whimpered Crall. "Kalidess has worked her sorcery on him."

The room went silent, and Stelia felt dread growing in the pit of her stomach. She wasn't ready to face Kalidess again. She didn't know if she ever would be.

Kalidess had spent years trying to twist Stelia to believe that she had rescued her from a bandit horde, when in reality Kalidess had set fire to Stelia's village herself, and sent the Drinaii to enslave any survivors. Stelia had caught her eye somehow, and had ended up in Kalidess's personal care, like a pampered pet, until she was of age to begin training. When she hadn't tested well for dark sorcery, Stelia had been sent into the Drinaii training camp. Her life went from one kind of waking nightmare to another. Years had gone by before she had been able to make her escape, and during those years she had done terrible things at Kalidess's command.

Stelia closed her eyes, as the Council continued, not able to think beyond a picture of Kalidess's face twisted in wrath. She knew what kind of punishments awaited for one of Kalidess's followers, especially the willing ones.

4 THE KING'S SECRET

Behind the closed door of his topmost tower room above his private quarters, King Alexandros stood staring into an archaic mirror rimmed with a rusty frame. The cracked glass was misted over as if he had fogged the glass with his breath, and he could barely make out his own haggard reflection and his sleep-deprived eyes.

Slowly, the fog cleared to reveal in multifaceted reflections of a beautiful, ageless woman with slitted pupils, and an oval face.

"King Alexandros," she hissed, forming her words perfectly with blood red lips, "Have you begun the battle?"

The King swallowed nervously, and made a shallow bow. "I have not, Dark Lady," he said, licking his dry lips. "I was waiting for your permission."

"You have had my permission for two weeks," she snapped. "I believe you wait for the safety of your son, whom you know takes lessons in the Sword Halls."

The King looked away, surprised. "You knew?"

"Of course," she growled softly. "I make it my business to know all that could upset my plans, as should you. Our deal is for you alone, not your son. You knew this, or why else would you drive him away?"

"He chooses not to be a part of my court," King Alexandros explained, trying to allay her suspicions.

"Your tastes in wine and entertainment are not his?" she asked archly.

"He doesn't understand that a King must have total control over his subjects, and undergoes more stresses than a normal man. Anyone under such stress should have all they need to relax." King Alexandros hands twitched nervously as he spoke.

"Of course," she said. "So if he disowned you, why do you wait, and save him?"

The King fingered the edge of his royal velvet robe. "I had a strange whim, following a strange dream." He tried not to shudder at the horror of his nightmare. The flames all around him, the screaming, the pain. They all felt like they were still within him.

"Dreams and visions are not always what they seem to be," she said quietly. "Your son, if he has been corrupted by the Triune Halls and their Lord, will never love you again. He will never appreciate the sacrifices you have made to gain vengeance and power over your enemies." Her lips curled in a small smile as she spoke of vengeance and power. The smile revealed sharp teeth.

King Alexandros looked down at the lush carpet in the room, not wanting to show his revulsion. His need for vengeance had created a foul alliance. After five years, he was beginning to doubt his wisdom in seeking out Kalidess's aid.

"I had merely hoped to have . . .someone to carry on my line after I am gone," he murmured. He kept his eyes down, wishing for a reprieve of some kind, but knowing that he must follow through with the course before him. He had made his choice.

"Of course, what parent doesn't wish that their child would follow in their footsteps?" Her eyebrows drew together, and she ran sharp nails over her chin. "Speaking of wayward children, have you news on that traitor Stelia?"

King Alexandros looked quickly over at the one window in this room. He felt trapped like a bird in a cage with a predator. "She serves the Triune Council as one of their scouts. She does not carry a sword of power."

"Of course, of course," Kalidess smiled again. "She would run to my family's enemy, and they wouldn't give her a sword of power with her background. They know she's mine." Then she said sharply, "Look at me, King Alexandros."

He dragged his eyes away from the window and back to her. He had been casting glances at her, but obviously that wasn't enough. He had to face down his uncomfortable ally. "What is it, Kalidess?"

"You must start the attack today. No more delays, or you will have broken your word, and you know what happens to those who break their word with me." She touched a small spot of scar tissue on her hand.

King Alexandros winced reflexively. She had already given him one lesson in her power. "I will start the attack, but first, I want to-

His words were cut off by a knock at his inner chamber door. Commander Raithan of the Drinaii Army, stepped into the room. He bowed low, but never quite lowered his eyes. His slick, greasy hair and strange metallic smell sickened King Alexandros. But he could not refuse the hand-picked servant of Kalidess.

King Alexandros made eye contact with Raithan and then flicked his eyes towards the mirror.

Raithan quickly followed the cue, and turned quickly to abase himself on his knees to the image of Kalidess. "Mistress, how may I serve you?" he whined.

"Convince the King to act faster than a Corlan snail," she snapped.

"Yes, your mistress," he said, standing to speak to the King. "Sire, you must attack at once." His dark eyes were inflamed with a passion to obey his dark mistress.

King Alexandros walked to the window, throwing the shutters open before turning again to speak to Kalidess and Raithan.

"Mistress, I ask just for one more hour," he said.

"The time is best now. Two of my men may have been followed last night," said Raithan.

"Sso, King Alexandros, you see that if we do not pounce at the right moment, the prey will escape, and if I do not get what I have asked for, you will not get what I promised."

"I thought that your men, your "shadow" Drinaii were capable of being undetected for months at a time, Raithan," said King Alexandros, throwing one of the man's prideful speeches back at him.

"Enough of this childish bickering and pleading for one more hour," said Kalidess. She held her finger up above a wrist for a moment.

Both men quailed, and King Alexandros felt sweat break out on his back.

"Yes, Dark Lady," he said, and he bowed slightly to her image. He trembled, knowing that if he openly delayed action any longer she would punish him, and he had already received one of her punishments. He must ensure that his son, however much he despised him, should get to safety. He owed that small thing to the memory of a boy who had once hidden under the ends of his royal train. He closed his eyes at the pain that surfaced in his chest.

"Send your men against the Triune Halls, as we discussed," said King Alexandros, hoping the Raithan followed the plans he had given them exactly.

"Yes, sire," Raithan said, "and the Hall housing scattered throughout the city?"

"Strike the Halls first, and then . . . round up the rest," said the King.

"As you wish, sire," said Raithan, his eyes glittering with some hidden pleasure. "Mistress, it is always my delight to serve your will," he said, groveling again.

King Alexandros repressed a shudder. He knew how repulsive some of Raithan's pleasures could be, based on the night court life. "Go," he said.

"As you command, your highness," snorted Rathan, as he left the chamber.

"Do not push my servant beyond his patience, or your kingdom will suffer unnecessarily," hissed Kalidess.

"Yes, Dark Lady," King Alexandros bowed again, and as he straightened, he watched her image dissolve into mist.

He sighed, and went to sit heavily down on his chair, letting his weight drop him deep into the cushions. He was in well over his head. The dark rage that had driven him to contact the Dark Sisterhood had simmered into despair.

The memory of his wife writhing in agony as the foreign poison of the Gyrriss flower worked its ways through her veins brought back a surge of his rage for a moment. It seemed strange that the Rryssori would be so blatant in their attack against his kingdom, using a plant known only to grow in their realm, but it was an evil act that needed an answer.

The dark sorceress had promised him power, a sword that would be more powerful than any the Sword Circle possessed; a sword of fire that he could use against the villains who had poisoned his wife.

But now his son was in danger, because of Kalidess's desire to wreak her own vengeance against the Triune Halls and the ward who had betrayed her. He hoped that somehow William would get out in time, and that his one remaining contact would be able to get him to safety.

5 DARKNESS FALLS

The wall sconces were already lit when Clara and Salene reached the practice rings in the cavernous old rooms under the Hall of the Sword. Salene started going through her forms, one after another with her sword strapped to her back. Clara started a few beats later, taking time to center herself on her own work. They were the two youngest apprentices to the Sword Masters, working their way through the cadet student classes within just seven years, instead of the usual ten. It wouldn't be long until Salene was invited to take the final trials for a senior apprenticeship and a crystal sword.

Their training wouldn't end with the entrance into the Chamber of Choice. No matter how good Clara or Salene had thought they had done, Master Dantor and Mistress Stelia could always show them ways to improve. If flawlessness was possible, then Master Dantor and Mistress Stelia were going to polish them to that end. Clara tried not to think about what it would mean to be a Champion, and let herself sink into the rhythm of her fighting patterns.

After several minutes of the basic warm up, she unsheathed her sword, and went through them again with the steel in her hands, keeping her distance from Salene who was doing the same. The only sound in the practice chamber was the sound of their breathing, and their boots on the stone floor beneath them.

When Clara finished her forms, she saw that Salene had already sheathed her sword and brought a pair of wooden practice swords from the rack. Clara grinned at Salene. "Ready to be pounded again?" she asked.

"Ready to pound some sense into your skull," replied Salene.

She threw one of the wooden blades to Clara, and Clara caught it easily.

"Wait!"

Clara turned to see Mistress Stelia coming towards them. She moved lithely, making no sound.

"Have you forgotten everything since I went on my scouting mission?" she asked them. It was her standard greeting the first time she watched them spar after being away.

Clara and Salene exchanged looks and rolled their eyes, grinning. "Yes, mistress," they said in sing-song voices.

Stelia gave them both stern looks, not longer joking. "You need to treat each bout seriously. If you are a true friend –

"you will fight like the worst enemies to help each other train," finished Salene and Clara.

Stelia threw up her hands, "ah, youth." Then she stepped into the circle with them, and gave them both a somber look. "Just because you've heard it before doesn't make it less true. What we do here can be fun, but it needs to be serious."

"Yes, Mistress Stelia," they both said.

Clara schooled her expression, and concentrated on the even stone floor for a moment. She must be like that stone, like the Crystal Swords that the Masters carried, unmovable and unbreakable, even by friendship. With a deep breath, she was ready.

As they engaged, Clara noted that Salene's eyes were narrowed, almost by her eyelids. She was tense, gripping her blade tight. As she began to step forward, Clara stepped back and slightly to her left, parrying with a smooth gesture, and coming in with a hop and a lunge that plunged her practice blade into Salene's leather chest-plate.

"Ouch," Salene said. She shook her head as she stepped back. "I don't know how you moved that fast and that hard, when I thought I had you."

"She read your movement and moved with you and then against you," Stelia stated. "Slow it down and repeat, so we can study the action."

As Clara and Salene took their places, and began the movements, Stelia gave pointers. "You were tense the first time, Salene, and that gave your attack away. Clara, you moved away when you really only had to move aside. That forced you to do that hop with your lunge earlier. Getting momentum in a fight isn't a bad thing, but you need to be more aware of the necessary distance for a parry and riposte. Again."

And so they practiced for at least a mark of time, and Clara relaxed into the rhythm of movement, balance, and distance that made sword fighting more like a dance than an effort. In the background, she began to notice a rumbling sound, and then she heard shouts. Clara stepped back, and Salene did as well, turning to Stelia. "What is it?" Clara asked.

Stelia's face paled, and then tightened. "Battle. Here in the halls, there is a battle." She pulled a helmet from the weapons rack, and motioned for them to follow her. At the base of the stairs she paused, and said tersely. "The King has made a deal with the Drinaii and they are in Skycliff disguised as Shadow Guards. We thought we had another day at least, but we were wrong. This battle will be more than anything you've ever trained for, but we can't leave the other students unprotected. Don't hold anything back."

Clara nodded, but Stelia didn't wait to see it. She drew her sword and ran up the stairs.

As she followed right behind Stelia, Clara felt her heart beating hard in her chest, and heard her breath gasping in her helmet. The shouts above them were loud, and there were cries of pain mixed with the crashing sounds of steel.

Two steps before the entryway, Stelia paused, and gave them the hand signal for "close," which meant stay close to her.

Clara tried to say something in response, but her throat would get any sound out. It was dry. She was drenched in sweat. Realizing belatedly that she still carried her practice sword, she threw it down and unsheathed her training sword. It might not be a sword of power, but it was good hard steel. On Stelia's signal, she followed her into the hall. Nearly deafened by the sound, Clara just stood there for a moment, shocked at the blood and the fighting. The Drinaii slaughtered everyone in their path. Sword Masters and apprentices fought a losing battle, outnumbered on three sides.

Stelia pointed to the right, where a group of Shepherd students crouched behind a reception desk, protected only by a single apprentice in gray. Clara didn't recognize him, but she knew he needed help. She pulled her sword out and began fighting her way to him. It wasn't like any practice bout she had ever encountered. She didn't take the time to size up her opponents. She just hacked, slashed, and kicked her way through them.

The first man she killed spit up blood as he slid down her sword onto the floor. Stelia put her boot on him, and helped Clara wrench the blade completely free. Clara felt sour bile sting her throat, but still she followed Stelia through the mayhem. Finally, they reached the sword apprentice and the Shepherd students.

At one point, she half-turned to see Salene guarding her back, fighting across the hall behind her. The path into the hall closed behind them, and they were soon surrounded with the other apprentice and the younger students.

Clara willed herself not to look at the faces of her opponents as she maimed and killed them in a frenzy of defense. After an age of battle, the space around them cleared for a moment. There were fights all over the hall, but not in front of their little group. Clara could see across the room for a moment.

Master Dantor, shadowed by four young students and Shepherd Jordan, worked his way across the room towards them. When the space cleared, he sent the students and the Shepherd running towards Stelia, and waved for them to go ahead.

The students' eyes were wide with fear, and many of them were crying. They were Shepherd and Law apprentices, and not trained for any of this. Shepherd Jordan swept past Clara in a blur of robes, and threw aside a tapestry behind them.

A narrow wooden door had been hidden there, and Shepherd Jordan ushered all the young students through it.

"Go," Stelia barked at Clara, Salene, and other sword apprentice.

Clara nodded, and backed towards the tapestry, trying to help Mistress Stelia for as long as she could. Stelia turned her head slightly and shouted at her one more time.

With her sword still drawn, Clara went through the door and took the tight spiral staircase down into the lower levels. There were few lanterns lit, and the passage felt close and hot.

Salene and the other apprentice stood near the edge of the stairs, close together, with their swords drawn. When they saw Clara, they drew apart slightly.

Salene looked up at the boy with a huge smile and said, "Thank the Lord she's safe."

Surprised that Salene obviously knew the apprentice when she didn't, Clara didn't know what to say.

Shepherd Jordan acknowledged her with a tense nod. "We have to get these young ones to safety, and these caverns will be overrun if the Hall is taken."

"Yes, sir," Clara and Salene answered promptly.

The boy stayed quiet, for a moment, and then said, "You are quite right, Shepherd Jordan. However, the only passages I know would be the wrong ones to take."

Clara wondered how he dared to take that tone with one of the Master Shepherds, but she didn't have time to confront him now.

Shepherd Jordan simply nodded, and then said, "I will take you as far as I know, and hope my memory will serve us well. When it does not, I will ask the Lord to guide us."

"Do you mean the hidden passages?" asked one of law students in light blue. He sniveled when he spoke, but he stood tall, like he was trying to be brave.

"Yes, have you studied them?" asked Shepherd Jordan.

"Yes, we always thought they were great places to look for pretend treasure. Me and James." The boy's face became downcast, and tears spilled onto his cheeks. "James is dead now." He wiped at his face. "But I can know the passageways as far as the green hall."

Shepherd Jordan put his arms around the boy for a moment. "Thank you, young Joseph. You will be of great help to me. Now, young ones, take hands, and let us go quickly now." He reached out and took Joseph's hand, who took another child's hand, and then another.

Salene and the other apprentice took places within the group of kids. When the last student, a girl of about nine or ten reached out to Clara, Clara just stood there. She had never been good with younger kids.

"I'll take the rear guard," she said. Her hands were streaked with the blood of her enemies that had run down her sword. The sight of it sickened her, and she hastily wiped it against a cleaning cloth from her belt pouch.

6 ENEMY AND FRIEND

Stelia and Dantor fought back to back. Stelia engaged three Drinaii at once, making sweeping cuts with her sword, and keeping her distance carefully.

Dantor reached around her in a quick move that sliced one of the Drinaii at the wrist. The Drinaii dropped his sword and stepped back. Dantor turned away again, engaging someone behind her.

Stelia fought the other two, baiting them until they both came at her at once, then she neatly ducked down and using a sword and dagger, she killed them both at once. As she pulled her blades free from the dying men, a Drinaii Captain sliced at her face.

She stumbled back into Dantor, then changed her direction with a roll, and swept his feet out from under him with a kick.

He rolled backwards and came up on his feet nimbly. Gazing at her intently, he saluted her with his sword. "I thought you were dead, Sarya Tellia, but I see that death cannot hold you."

She brought the edge of her sword to Jennar's neck. She realized that she hadn't recognized him when he attacked because of a new scar that split the right side of his face from temple to chin. "You left me for dead," she hissed at him. "and the woman I was is dead. Now, go, before I forget we were friends once." She kicked him in the ribs and he staggered away, dropping his sword completely to the floor. Then she turned to see Dantor dispatch his last opponent.

"Time for us to follow our students," he said.

Stelia glanced around her and saw that nearly all those who stood for the Triune Halls were dead, or surrounded. She nodded to Dantor, and grabbing his arm, she pushed aside the tapestry, and pulled him after her down into circular stairway.

Dantor slid the locking bar into place behind them, and they hurried down the steps.

"You knew that man," he said as the sounds of battle receded behind them.

"I did," she said quietly, wishing her past didn't exist. She let go of her grip on him, and concentrating on moving quickly down the tight spiral staircase.

"He was, a friend? A close friend?"

Stelia tried to figure out how to say what she needed to say without having to return to her memories of the past. "Drinaii soldiers don't have friends, but we were . . . close. Very close." A shadow of a memory flashed in her mind . . .running through meadow of tall grass, laughing. One of the few times she remembered laughing as a child. And then another memory, a warm breath on her cheek. This memory was replaced swiftly by another: the sight of Jennar riding away with his back to her as she struggled against the bonds that held her trapped against the scorching sands of the desert. She stopped for a moment, and put her hand on the cool wall next to her. "I can't talk about it now."

"It's all right," said Dantor. "Well, except we need to keep moving so your former friends don't kill us."

"Except that," Stelia said, almost smiling at the irony in rich voice. She started moving again, running lightly down the stairs.

At the bottom, they ran towards the seawall side of the passage, and soon came up against Clara, bristling with two throwing knives in her hands, prepared to defend the others behind her. When she saw them, she re-sheathed her knives, and let her shoulders droop. "Thank the Lord, it's you," she said.

"Yes, thank the Lord, and unexpected friends," said Dantor, giving Stelia's arm a small squeeze.

Stelia nodded at him, not trusting her voice.

"The others are just up ahead," Clara said.

7 UNDER SKYCLIFF

With a torch in her hand, Clara could see just in a small circle around her, and the torch in front of her, carried by the apprentice she didn't recognize. For some reason, the adults treated him with deference. The others were shadowy shapes in the darkness. After attempting to plant several false trails, they had descended further under the Triune Halls into the oldest parts of Skycliff.

Clara startled at the feel of a small hand touching the side of her that carried the torch, and she looked down into the soft gray eyes of the little girl. "Can I walk by you?"

Clara turned slightly to see Stelia out of the corner of her eye.

Stelia nodded her head, and said, "Keep the torch, but at the first sign of trouble, you'll need to let go of the girl, and take up your sword again."

"All right," she said, nodding grimly. Then she looked down at the little girl as she sheathed her sword. "I'll hold your hand now, if you would like that. But at the first hint of trouble, I want you to let go and run until you reach Shepherd Jordan."

The girl quickly switched sides and took hold of her right hand. Her thin little fingers were clammy to the touch, and she shivered. At first, Clara felt awkward holding the girl's hand, but after a while she began to find it almost comforting.

The light of the torch seemed feeble compared the heavy darkness that surrounded them, and they walked on for what seemed like hours, or merely tense minutes. Clara couldn't be sure. The disorientation of the darkness, the flickering torches, and the horror of the fight behind her, kept Clara from knowing the passage of time. The little hand in hers seemed to be keeping her from flying apart.

Next to her, Stelia was quiet except for her steady, slowing breath. Slowly, Clara realized that the girl must be getting tired, for she pulled down on Clara's hand now, and her steps were getting slower.

"Are you all right?" Clara asked her.

"Just tired, and scared, and tired of being scared," the girl answered, her voice rising in pitch as she spoke.

Clara leaned down, and said, "I can carry you for a little while, in front," she said, using her free arm like a sling in the front of her body. The girl's dark curls rested against her cheek.

"I want my mommy," the girl said in a sob. "She's soft when she holds me," she said, as way of explanation.

"Armor is never good for affection," Clara said. "My mom wanted to make me wait until she took hers off, before she would hold me. But I always wanted to launch myself at her as soon as she came in the room, even with her hard leathers."

"Is she your mom?" asked the girl, nodded her head towards Stelia.

Stelia shook her head. "Heavens no, child. I've never been fit to be a mother." Her face took on a grim expression, and then she seemed to force a smile. "Although I am honored to be Clara's mentor."

"Thank you," said Clara, smiling at Stelia briefly. She allowed herself a vision of her mother, striding through the sunlight along the outer wall in her full armor. "My mother is a sword master like Stelia, but she's a guard and not a scout," she said. It didn't seem like enough of a description. "She has blue eyes like the sky, and hair that looks like spun gold, and her hands, even calloused, are gentle and kind."

"My mom has soft hands," said the girl. "She's a baker. She wakes up early in the morning before it gets hot, and bakes the most delicious bread in Skycliff. And my Dad, he's a shoemaker, and likes to work early too. Our house is above their shops, and we have a roof garden above that."

"That sounds a little like my home," said Clara, "except we live above an instrument shop, near the northern edge of the city. Our roof has a garden too."

Clara went silent thinking back to the morning. She wondered if she would ever see her parents again. She swallowed slowly, trying to hold back tears. Her mother's smile, and her father's hug seemed so far away now.

The little girl broke the silence. "My name's Helena."

"I'm Clara." She wondered at how their voices seemed to warm the cold darkness around them, and suddenly she hoped that their conversation would just continue for as long as the walk in the darkness lasted.

"Is your Dad a sword master too? Are you all sword masters?"

"No," Clara said. "He's a Shepherd like you. He's tall and lean, and full of music. He's one of the teachers at the Triune Halls this year, you may even know him. He's Master Ferrald."

"I've heard of him, the trouble triplets even like him."

"The trouble triplets?" Clara asked.

"They're new students this year," Helena said, "and full of trouble and talent, Shepherd Jordan says. They are up there with Master Dantor, but they're being good now."

"Good," Clara said, hoping that these so-called trouble triplets would be wise enough to follow instructions until they were free and safe.

"Thanks for carrying me," said Helena, and she lay her head completely on Clara's shoulder and let herself relax her full weight.

Clara settled into a looser version of her normal walk, bending her knees more to take the impact of the heaviness of the little girl. When she had first picked up Helena, she had been a barely noticeable weight. Now, Clara felt herself tiring.

Finally, as she rounded a sharp curve in the passageway, she saw the others had stopped at a huge stone door that blocked the passageway. Salene knelt on the stone floor, holding two children and singing a soft song.

Clara felt glad that Salene had such a good way with kids. Although she was only an apprentice, Salene had already spent time teachings some the younger ones in training sessions. Clara always felt clumsy around kids, although Helena seemed to be all right.

Dantor and the other apprentice were pushing on the door, while Shepherd Jordan inspected the hinges.

Clara put Helena down. "I need to help them," she said.

"Thanks, Clara," Helena said, and then she went to sit with Salene.

Clara helped shove the door open, digging her feet into the stone floor beneath them, and heaving on the counts that Dantor gave.

The door opened slowly, inching forward, until they could each squeeze through it.

Stelia came last, and then helped close the door.

Clara noticed a heavy wooden beam sitting by the side of the door. "We're lucky the latch wasn't closed," she said.

"Luck has nothing to do with life," said Shepherd Jordan. "The Lord opened the way for us."

"And now we can shut it on our enemies," said Dantor.

"He leads us to green pastures," said Stelia reverently, gazing beyond them.

Clara took her torch from Shepherd Jordan to gaze around with wonder. They had entered a cavernous room that sparkled with thousands of green gems embedded in the walls. Across the room sat a dais, and cutting through the center of the room, a small stream trickled over gem encrusted rocks.

"What is this place?" she whispered.

"The Green Hall," said one of the students. "The throne room of King Wilstorm, the first King of Septily."

"In all my escapades, I never searched out the underground of Skycliff," Clara admitted.

"We would have done it eventually," Salene said. Then she walked over to a trough that ran around the length of the room. "Look, it's torch gas."

The other sword apprentice dipped his torch into the trough, and it lit a blaze of burning oil and light that swept the length of the trough and around the room.

The green gems sparkled with brilliance, and Clara realized that they were crystals, like those in a crystal sword of power. Back by the door, she grabbed a dousing cap and doused her torch. The younger students, Shepherd Jordan, and the apprentice she didn't know went to the stream and began to wash in its flow.

Before she went to join them, she turned to Salene. "Who is he? That apprentice? You seem to know him, but I don't."

"He's a liability," Salene said grimly.

8 A LIABILITY

"And here I thought you had affection for our young Prince," said Dantor, obviously surprised by Salene.

"Prince?!" Clara asked. She felt her voice rising in pitch and volume, but she didn't try to stop herself. She clenched her hands in fists as she spoke. "Prince, like the King's Son, the Prince? How can we trust him? Are you sure he isn't leaving signs so the King's Guard can slaughter us?"

"He warned us of their arrival and their attack. How does that serve the King or the King's Shadow Drinaii?" Master Dantor asked. "Besides he's been a student of mine for nearly as long as you have been."

"It could be a part of a subtle plot to betray us at our worst moment," Clara said, ignoring the fact that she held Master Dantor's perceptions of people highly.

"William would not do that," Salene said, "His father put him aside for other pursuits about five years ago. William . . . is not the pampered noble, or loyal royalist that you might imagine," Salene said.

"Then why did you state that he is a liability?"

"The Drinaii will not rest until they have found him, and killed him," Salene said, frowning. "If we were here, just as students, apprentices, and Masters, they might ignore our escape. But with him with us, they will find us, or die trying. Their mistress will kill them if they don't fulfill her commands."

"And what do you know of their mistress?" Dantor asked.

"What mistress? Don't you mean the King?" Clara asked at the same time.

"My former mistress, Kalidess," stated Stelia, coming up to join them.

"The King has allied himself with Kalidess?" Clara knew she was just repeating the others words but she couldn't seem to help herself. The shock of the whole day seemed to be pressing down on her, the reality of the bloodshed, the precarious nature of their escape. She wanted to sit down and weep, or scream, or hit something. She wasn't sure which. Or maybe just cover her head with her hands and close her eyes against all of it.

"I discovered the alliance just last night," said Stelia quietly. "I had suspected it, and the Prince has been trying to gain information without being caught, but the pieces fell into place too late for us to change the course of events."

She reached forward and put a hand on Clara's arm. "They will not let us rest long. We need to clean our swords, discover the secrets of this Green Hall if they will help us, and then move on quickly." With a gentle tug, she pulled Clara towards the stream.

Clara followed numbly, feeling as if the place couldn't be real, the prince couldn't be real, the Drinaii couldn't be real. She must be having some kind of nightmare. Soon she would wake up again in her own bed, and start a better day.

The shocking cold of the stream against her skin woke her to reality. She watched the blood wash away from her hands and sword in the water that flowed gently over green gems and dark rocks into a dark tunnel blocked by a mossy grate.

"Stelia, how can I be the next Champion when the sight of blood, and the act of killing sickens me?" she asked quietly.

Stelia didn't respond for a moment, but simply rubbed her sword dry with a cloth. "Those who are called to protect do not walk an easy path." She sighed. "I have killed more than you will ever kill in your lifetime, Clara. I have been a monster, and yet, the Lord still has a use for me. I tried to give up my sword for a while, but this work," she held up the weapon, "it is a part of me that I understand in a way that goes beyond anything else." She gazed at Clara intently. "To feel as you do is a blessing, and not a curse. You understand the sanctity of life, and you have the ability to protect others. There will always be those who do not feel as you do, who will be bent on a path of destruction. Your skills are needed."

Clara nodded. "But I don't like them much, now that I've seen . . . well, what we saw in the halls."

"I know." Stelia sighed again. "I don't either, but I have worse memories to bear."

"What about the others, Salene and Prince William? Why do they seem ok?"

"You know the answer to that," Stelia said. "They've seen it before. This isn't their first time."

"Salene's brother," whispered Clara, remembering him and the night he died. Shortly after Salene's father, Lord Gray had been stripped of his office as a Governor of the Desert District, assassins had entered the Gray home with an intent to kill the entire family. Salene had protected herself, and her father and mother's bodyguards had protected them, but Salene's brother Caleb had died. Salene had been only nine. Clara remembered not understanding why her friend didn't want to do any sword work for several weeks after that. She had been such an unfeeling fool. "I didn't know."

"No, but you do now, and the Prince has his own past. Life in the palace these last seven years has not been easy."

Clara nodded. "I've heard." Rumors of bear baiting, duels over noble ladies, and other tasteless pursuits had pervaded Skycliff. The King had lost the respect of his people a long time before the attack.

But not all Kings went bad, this Hall stood as testimony to that. The stones of the Hall were dark but covered in green crystals that bathed the room in a verdant glow. Green crystals were associated with healing, and weren't usually found in swords, but in the hands of

Shepherds and Lawgivers. King Wilstorm had held a green sword, a green staff, and a green scepter in the legends.

The dais and the throne were actually the plainest features in the room, not carved or covered in crystals like the rest of the Great Green Hall. Clara watched as the Prince knelt down at the foot of the dais as if he were praying.

She had only seen King Alexandros from afar during a feast day celebration, but his angry demeanor had been noticeable in his stance and features even from a distance. This prince seemed young and even unsure.

Salene crossed the stream and went to him, putting her hand on his shoulder. Clara watched them with the sinking realization that here was proof of her long held suspicions; she had thought that Salene was keeping something from her. Their friendship had changed since they entered Septily. It changed when Salene's brother had died, and it changed every year, but lately Salene had been busier, distracted by something that she didn't share with Clara. She knew that people changed when they got older, but she didn't want to lose her friendship with Salene. She rose from her place by the stream, and crossed it easily with a small jump.

Approaching Salene and the prince, she listened to their conversation.

"He hasn't acknowledged me in years. How can I be the prince of Septily?" The prince said.

"You are, and you will be King," said Salene, her tone confidant and reassuring.

The prince sighed.

Clara tripped over a loose stone in the floor.

Salene and the prince turned, and Clara noticed how Salene seemed ready to defend him, standing half a step between them, and putting her hand out. Clara bit her lip and didn't know what to say.

The prince stood up, and put his hand on Salene's arm. "It's all right, Salene," he said. "You must be Clara, Salene's best friend, and the next Champion of Septily. I'm William."

"Prince William," Salene said.

"Nice to meet you . . . Prince William," Clara said.

"My friends call me Will, but I only have a few friends," he said, looking down at the ground. He looked up again, and his green eyes seemed deep and intense in the light of the green gems around them. "I would like it if we could be friends, Clara. I feel like I already know you from Salene's tales of your escapades."

Clara bit her lip again, frustrated that Salene had never mentioned her friendship with this prince, but he had given her an opening and she decided to go with it. She half-smiled and chuckled a little. "Did she tell you about the time we borrowed keys from the High Justice's office?"

"That was clever, how you used his cat to distract him," Will said, smiling as if he had been there too.

They all laughed softly together, and then Clara looked away.

"It seems wrong to laugh, doesn't it?" said Salene, grimacing.

"It does," Clara said, "and yet, this place," she raised her hands and circled looking around the room, "it feels good here, safe."

Stelia walked over and interrupted them. "We need to prepare to leave. No matter how safe it feels, Kalidess's forces are clever enough to penetrate it."

"Safe for nearly a thousand years, and now soon to be overrun by forces of evil. It seems impossible that such a thing could happen to Skycliff, or the Green Hall." Prince William looked solemn. "My father has been walking down the path of vengeance and bitterness, but I never realized he would betray his own people and his own country."

"I'm sure that he didn't realize the extent of his bargain with Kalidess until it was too late," said Stelia softly.

"But you escaped her. It's possible to change your path," said Prince William.

"It is possible, but I didn't strike a bargain with her. I was her slave, and then her servant. She twisted me until . . .I believed in her. She never sealed my service with a formal bargain. Those are harder to break," said Stelia heavily.

Prince William put his hands over his face. "O Lord, have mercy on my father," he said quietly.

Salene put her arm around him, and laid her head against his shoulder, giving him wordless comfort.

Clara just stood there, feeling alone in a room full of people.

9 DOOR TO DESTINY

"Hallelujah!" Shepherd Jordan shouted out, breaking Clara's melancholy thoughts. He waved at everyone to come join him, and Clara joined the others gathering around him.

"I have found another door, one marked by the symbol of the Trinity and the Triune Halls," he stated.

Helena wormed her way through the crowd to press up against Clara. "I want you to hold my hand again," she said.

"All right," Clara said, realizing that it might not be so bad to have Helena tagging along beside her.

Shepherd Jordan used his staff to show the faint outlines of a door that matched the walls around it. The symbol of the trinity was set in such a way that it looked like a wall carving. "Beyond this door we will most likely find a chamber. Either this chamber will be an old meeting place, or it will be a place of great treasure, or it will be a place of refinement."

He looked at each of them in turn, and as his gaze rested on Clara, she felt excitement rise with the pounding of her heart. The only two places she knew with this symbol in the Triune Halls above them were the Council Chamber, and the Chamber of Swords where the new Sword Masters chose their Crystal Swords. Each master spoke of their blade as if it were a part of their very soul. In the legends, only the purest of heart could bear the blade of True Crystal, a blade made solely of Crystal alone. Those were the blades reserved for

Champions, but Clara didn't feel worthy of that honor.

"It could be a Scroll Chamber," said Helena excitedly.

"Or a chamber of weights and measures," said one of the Law apprentices.

Clara remembered belatedly that each Hall had its own special chambers, and hoped that somehow it would meet all their expectations.

"Shepherd Jordan, are you sure they are ready for this?" Master Dantor asked.

"The Maker knows their hearts, and he will give them what they need; forgiveness, strength, patience, faith . . .he never tests us beyond bearing, but always gives us exactly what we need to trust in Him."

Stelia looked as if she would interrupt Shepherd Jordan but then she bit her lip, and rested her weight on one leg, looking over at Clara.

Was that a worried look, or a warning, or what? Clara didn't know. Stelia's face could sometimes be unreadable. She hoped that Stelia would finally accept a blade of power.

Shepherd Jordan turned and traced his fingers over the symbols on the door. "It is best opened by three of the three halls," he said, then he turned to Master Dantor. "You are the top sword master here, and will stand for the sword, while I stand for the spirit, and Prince William as senior Law-giver, you will stand for the Law, come."

Behind her Prince William stirred and their little group parted to let him through. Next to Master Dantor, and Shepherd Jordan, he looked tall and extremely young. Master Dantor was just younger than middle age, and Shepherd Jordan was into his active senior years, but Prince William looked like a boy next to them. His face held sorrow, but his brown eyes looked like those of a lost puppy, and his brown hair seemed suddenly shaggy in comparison to Master Dantor's dark, cropped hair and Shepherd Jordan's flowing white mane. He didn't look like a king, or at least not like his father, Clara realized. She relaxed at the thought. She still couldn't see whatever it was that Salene obviously saw in him, but she could see that he was clean, in a way that his father was not.

Shepherd Jordan tipped his staff forward in the semi-circle created by the three men. Then Prince William took a small book out of his breast pocket and held it up towards the center. Dantor looked at them both, and reached up to draw his Crystal Sword from its sheath.

Everyone's attention seemed focused on Dantor's hand as he drew the crystal blade out of his pommel. The younger students gasped as they noticed the color of the crystal running up the center of the blade, and in the stones that inlaid the pommel, even the steel of the blade seemed to hold the dark color of the crystal.

"It's black like midnight," Helena said in surprise.

"Yes," Master Dantor said. "I was a very angry young master when I entered the testing chamber. The Maker tested my soul and my heart, and knew I needed to carry a black blade to remind me of my pride, and to delve into the depths when it is needed."

Shepherd Jordan started to chant. "Three in one, and one that is three, Maker, Savior, Spirit, be in us as we see."

Out of the staff, a glow radiated over the room, highlighting the crystal facets in the walls, and sending shimmers of light over all of them. The book that Prince William held opened in his hand, and a rich creamy color joined the glow of the staff. Dantor's blade shimmered like moonlight on water.

Shepherd Jordan bowed his head, and everyone else followed suit. "Lord, mighty Maker of the universe of our very inmost beings, forgive us for our sins, and guide us in your light. Give us the strength needed to endure the trials that the evil one has set before us, and refine us with your living presence. Amen."

"Amen," said Clara, along with the others.

The door opened softly, despite being a heavy stone slab. As the others entered, Clara could hear their whispers of awe and excitement, and could see a rainbow of colors reflecting from their torches. As she reached the door, peering in at what seemed to be a treasure room, Master Dantor put his hand on her shoulder.

"Clara, the Lord has shown me this place in my vision. You will be tested alone, and you will be His light. Place all your trust in Him, and you will be His light." He gave her shoulder a squeeze. "May His blessing be upon you," he said. Then he gave her a gentle push.

Clara stumbled over the doorway, and into darkness, falling into complete emptiness. She screamed, but the inky blackness swallowed her voice. Cold air pushed against her as she continued to fall downward, and she struggled against it, clawing to one side and then another, searching for a wall, a handhold, anything.

Nothingness surrounded her. She began to wonder why she hadn't hit the bottom of this place yet, and what had happened to the others. The air rushing against her seemed to slow, and she spread her arms again. She was floating, almost flying, still moving downward but slower, more gracefully.

"Praise the Lord," she said softly.

Her toes lightly touched a surface beneath her, and she gently came down onto a hard, rocky surface. She still couldn't see anything, and her ears felt muffled by the silence. She couldn't smell anything other than her own sweat, and the strange scent of blood on her clothes.

She pulled her shield forward from its harness on her back. Protected as well as she could be, she waited, feeling her muscles grow tight with tension. Something had to happen soon.

Time went by. She didn't know how much, but the sweat on her back cooled, and she still waited. She didn't understand what was happening, and where the others were, but she guessed that she was being tested. It made sense, given that the masters never spoke of their time in the Chamber of Choice, if this was a chamber like that. The Word often spoke of trials, tests, and temptations.

She thought she had passed the first one. She didn't understand this one. It gave her too much time to think, to wonder if the others were already finished with their tests, if her parents were alive, if the other refugees had reached it to safety and how many there were.

She realized suddenly that she hadn't felt for the walls since she had landed on the ground. She stood slowly, and hesitatingly reached out first one direction and then another. Nothing. She walked forward seven paces and felt nothing, then back fourteen paces, then to the sides, and back to her starting point. Nothing seemed to surround her, and the sound of her footsteps died away without echoing back. The eeriness, and loneliness began to worm its way into her, and she began to feel afraid.

Her breath started to come in short, shaky gasps, and finally, she took a slow, deep breath, and then another. She bowed her head, and prayed, "O Lord, I need you in this darkness. I feel so alone, and yet I know you are with me. Please, Lord, let me see your light. Amen."

As she opened her eyes, a soft glow grew around her. The walls of the chamber were wider than she had dared to travel, and the light seemed to be coming from all directions. The room seemed to start spinning, with light and colors all around her: reds, blues, greens, yellows, browns, purples, pinks, greys, and whites. They swirled and swirled, and yet she stood still, dizzied by the display.

She closed her eyes for a moment, and when she opened them again, she was surrounded by swords on all sides, hanging from the walls in vast numbers, glowing with light. The light seemed to grow in intensity, building slowly to a bright white that peaked in strength in the center of the room, just a step away from Clara.

Her eyes watered, but she didn't look away. She felt afraid, and yet awed by the wonder of the sight, and she didn't care if she were blinded, she only knew she had to look at the light.

Slowly, the light receded again, and she could see a single sword, hanging in the air, a sword of pure white, of light and truth. She longed for it, and without meaning to she reached out for it, her fingers slowly winding their way around the smooth pommel.

When her grip became solid, it warmed in her hands, and she felt a presence touch her soul, the presence of the Lord. All thoughts, all feelings, all doubts and fears, all worries, and all strivings ceased. She simply stood in the presence of the Lord, in warmth, light, peace, truth, and love.

10 TREASURE

In the crystal treasure chamber, Stelia walked around the room, feeling dazzled by the crystals, but worried about Clara. The girl had disappeared in a flash of light, and although Dantor assured her that he had seen a vision of this, that Clara would be all right, she prowled the room looking for any evidence of dark sorcery.

She noticed the door behind them had been left open to the Green Hall. Once she had closed the door behind them, she had a momentary misgiving that Clara might need that entrance. She decided to wait by the door.

As she stood there, she slowly relaxed, letting down some of her guard. The room seemed to brighten in response, and she looked over the contents of the room with wonder. It was a treasure house of crystalline armor and weaponry. There were staves, swords, scales, scrolls, lamps, shields, hauberks, greaves, helmets, belts, and even leather sandals that looked like the sturdy ones of the old Empire . . . still found intact after a thousand years of disuse.

Next to her Stelia discovered a set of light mail, made of a silvery metal that glinted as she picked it up in her hands. The weave of the metal was soft and yet tough, harder than anything she had expected. Near it, lay a large shield. Stelia longed to pick it up, but she restrained herself. Her past made her unworthy to carry such armor.

Yet, she was reluctant to put down the mail, and as she stood, debating with her longing and her hopes, a light grew all around her until she found herself surrounded by whiteness.

In that moment time seemed to slow, and she could hear a soothing baritone voice, speaking to her.

"Sarya called Stelia, I have paid your price," said the voice lovingly.

In the bright whiteness she could see for a moment a hand pierced with a nail, and she bowed her head. "I am not worthy of such sacrifice."

"You are my child and I gladly paid the price so that you could turn to me, not just halfway, but fully. Please, Sarya called Stelia, come and throw yourself in my arms, trust in me, and take up my weapons for my glory."

"I will, gracious Lord," Stelia said. "I will," she repeated, feeling a tear slide down her cheek. When she opened her eyes again, she stood exactly where she had been before the vision.

"Are you all right?" asked Dantor, suddenly at her side. His eyes were tight with concern, and he reached out his hand to her face, and then dropped it.

Stelia nodded and looked at the mail shirt in her hands, "I received a vision. I think I will be more than all right," she said awkwardly.

"Good," said Dantor. His dark brown eyes relaxed, and he looked down at the mail shirt in her hands. "That is some fine mail," he said, reaching out his hand to touch it.

Their fingers brushed, and Stelia fought the urge to bolt from the tingly feeling she felt that started in her fingers and ran through her. "Dantor," she said quietly.

"Yes," he said, bowing his head closer to hers.

"I should probably tell you that Stelia isn't my real name . . . in case, anything happens to me," she added.

"I didn't think it could be, although it mostly suits you." He smiled warmly at her. "Although you are a woman of steel strength, I know there is more to you than that."

Stelia felt warmth in her cheeks, and hoped he couldn't tell that she was blushing. "Sarya is my name, but I would ask that you not call me that until we finish the sorceress."

"I will keep it safe," said Dantor, winding his fingers around hers.

Stelia looked down at their hands, and became completely still, holding onto the wonder of the moment. Then she wriggled her fingers away from his, and he let her go. "You don't know everything about my past, Dantor."

She felt his warm hand on her cheek, and he said gently, "You are a remarkable woman now, and the past is behind you."

His deep chocolate brown eyes gazed at her warmly, and his gentle smiling lips looked soft. Stelia sucked in a short breath, and then the moment was broken by a small hand on her arm.

"Master Dantor, Mistress Stelia," interrupted Rodhrie at their elbow.

"Yes," said Dantor, letting go of Stelia's hand.

"I . . . I, I had a vision, and this armor, it was a part of it," he said, looking both elated and nervous. He wore an amazing set of armor, made of sky blue crystal and light metal, with a sword that matched at his side, along with a scroll case, a stave, and an impressive shield. It seemed slightly big on him, but he was at an age of growth. "I don't understand," he said, "I'm a law student, not a sword student."

"It happens sometimes that the Lord chooses us for more than one task, and more than one area. It means that we have extra studies, and extra work in front of us," Dantor said sternly.

"Shepherd Jordan said that it might be a sign, that I will have what I need as time comes," said Rhodrie, looking a little overwhelmed.

"It's all right, Rhodrie," said Stelia, "I think that Prince William will put your fears to rest. He has handled all three in secret for five years now, so I believe that you will be able, and the Lord will make your path clear each step of your journey."

"Exactly," said Dantor. "Let's go speak to him together."

"I need to . . . put on the armor that the Lord has provided," said Stelia.

"Yes," said Dantor, "I received this . . ." he held up a stave, "and this," he held up a new shield. "The gifts of the Lord are light and true." The armor Dantor wore every day was his crystal armor, but most did not notice because the crystal was only a subtle part of the design, and the metal was dark and not polished.

"We will speak again," he promised Stelia, with a glow in his eyes, and then he turned to Rhodrie and led the boy across the room to Prince William.

Stelia watched him for a moment, watching his steady purposeful movements. He walked like a deadly fighter and a graceful dancer at the same time.

She bent to pick up the armor meant for her. She marveled at the lightness and flexibility of each piece, and how well it fit her. The mail shirt, metal breastplate, belt, greaves, helmet, and even new leather boots all seemed to be fitted exactly to her measurements. The sword, when she lifted it felt like a rich and steady presence in her hand, glowing with a mild amber color.

As she admired it, the center of the treasure room flashed bright, and when the light receded, Clara stood there, holding a clear blade, the blade of a Champion. Stelia sheathed her own blade and went to speak to her.

11 FRIENDS

Clara opened her eyes and saw that she was no longer alone. Salene stood at her side, in a chamber filled with swords, scrolls, staffs, and armor, all glowing with crystals.

Salene, herself, glowed with radiance. In her hands, she held a sword with a line of purple crystal intertwined around the hilt and running up the center of the blade. On her chest she wore a breastplate of gold, with the tree and the circle on it, the symbol of the Savior and the Creator, with a dove flying out of the tree – the Spirit.

"You disappeared, and then there was this light, and your sword . . . it's the one sword, the Sword of Truth," Salene said with wonder. Then she smiled even broader. "You are the Champion."

"I am," said Clara, quietly, gazing at the sword in her hands. Perfectly balanced in her grip, the sword glowed with light from within the crystal. The gold pommel seemed to have a perfect counterweight for the blade, and fit her hands like it was made for her. She held it out away from her at shoulder height and it felt like an extension of her arm.

The rest of their group of refugees gathered around her, and she lowered her weapon, and then turned it so that she held it on the palms of her hands. She knelt in the midst of them. "I pledge my heart, my mind, my soul, my body, and this blade to the Lord, to the Triune Halls, and to the people of Septily. We will take our home back from the darkness, and free our people."

She looked up at Prince William, and then bowed her head again. "As long as you uphold the ways of the Lord, I will serve you as the Prince of our people, and rightful ruler of our land."

"I accept your service, Champion Clara," said Prince William. He reached out his hand, and placed it on top of hers over the cross guard of her blade. "We will serve the Triune Halls and Septily together."

"For the Lord's glory."

Everyone around them raised their swords, or scrolls, or staffs and shouted, "Amen!"

The sound of their voices echoed in the chamber.

Clara noticed that each person had been gifted with something from the chamber. The lawgiver students held scrolls with glowing words. The Shepherd students held staffs and scrolls, Salene and Prince William had new armor, and Salene held a purple crystal sword in her hands. Then she noticed Helena and another boy standing next to Shepherd Jordan, loaded down with various items: armor, blades, scrolls, and short staves that strapped to their sword belts. They had been triple gifted, and her heart went out to them, as they both looked slightly overwhelmed and awed.

"There is more for you, as well, Champion Clara," said Master Dantor at her side. "Every Champion is gifted not only with the True Sword, but with gifts from all three areas of the Triune Halls. I think if you walk this chamber, you will find the ones that are meant for you, and some new armor as well."

Clara looked at him and smiled wryly. "Will that just mean more lessons, Master?"

"Of course," he said, smiling widely. "Just because the Lord has chosen you to be Champion doesn't mean the lessons are over."

"But the lessons may be a little more experiential than before," said Stelia in her husky voice, with a note of warning. Her eyes looked sad as well as proud, as she looked at Clara. Her armor was new as well, and she seemed to glow in the cavern's subdued light.

"I understand, Master Stelia," said Clara. Then she took Master Dantor's advice and walked around the room, letting a tingling sense of rightness guide her first to a set of armor on one side of the room, a set of short staves that clipped to the back of her sword belt in another area, and a tiny scroll inside a pouch.

The scroll glowed faintly with bright light, and she opened it slowly to read just these words, "I can do all things through Him who strengthens me." She savored the words for a moment, and then re-rolled the tiny strip of paper, replaced it in its holder and placed it in a small pocket on her shirt under her armor and next to her heart.

Across from her, Salene studied her own small scroll, but when she caught Clara's gaze, she wrapped it back up and placed it in her pouch. "We have to talk, Clara, about William."

"You love him," Clara said.

Salene blushed bright red. "Clara," she whispered. "I don't, well, I might, but we're both really young."

"You're fifteen and he's eighteen, alliances have been made at those ages before," Clara said pragmatically.

"I thought you would be . . .well, upset," Salene said.

Clara stood there for a moment, and looked up at the ceiling, feeling as if the world had been switched around too far, and wondering if anything would feel normal again. "I just worry that somehow we'll never be the same again. I mean, I know we won't be, but I don't want to lose your friendship."

"You haven't," Salene said, her face becoming serious. "We will always be friends."

"I know. I just wish . . . we were still kids in the desert." Clara hugged Salene, trying to hide the tears forming in her eyes. She really wished that she could be a kid again, that they didn't have to grow up. She didn't want her relationships to change, or at least not her friendship with Salene. But everything had changed, and although she was the Champion, she was powerless to stop it all.

Letting go of Salene, she watched Prince William approach them, and she stepped away from the two of them, and bumped into

Helena.

"Look, Clara," she said, with excitement in her eyes. "I received a crystal sword too, and I'm a shepherd student. But I also have a pair of staves, and a scroll, and armor. Shepherd Jordan says that I have a lot of learning to do, but I'll be expected to great things. What do you think? Do you think it's possible we could go fight the Drinaii right now, and take back our city?"

"With God, anything is possible," Clara said, but then she looked around the room at their small group and continued, "however, I think we might want a few more allies to make an impression on the Drinaii. They have a huge army."

"Yes, we need allies," said Shepherd Jordan, coming over to join their conversation. "I have contacts that will aid us as soon as we leave these caverns, and we will need to do that soon. Although this chamber is hidden from those of evil intent, we do not want to let the Drinaii block us from our exit."

"What kind of contacts?" asked Clara.

"The Watch Guard," said Shepherd Jordan.

Clara nodded, remembering them from her history lessons. They were an elusive people, who felt it their duty to watch over the lands of Aramatir and help those fleeing from dark forces. They didn't usually take an active role in any battle, but Clara trusted the Shepherd Jordan knew those that would help them.

12 POISON

King Alexandros nervously paced the dais of his empty throne room. Courtiers were all in their rooms, or away in their houses. He had closed court while he awaited news from the Drinaii. So far, he had heard nothing, and hours had passed.

He feared for his son's safety, but he had no one he could trust to speak to about his son. His son's supporters were his enemies. He had planned it that way when he first began to get a glimmer of the extent of Kalidess's evil and of her reach, but now it filled him with a hollow dread instead of a sense of hope. He had wanted revenge for his wife's death and had made a deal with Kalidess. He rubbed at the scar on his wrist worriedly. Once the deal had been made, he could see no way out but to protect his son by pushing him away.

Across from him, the doors were flung open, and King Alexandros turned quickly to scowl at the Drinaii guard captain who was so rude not to knock.

"Do you not give honor to your King?" he snarled as the man approached.

"Sire, I apologize" the man said with a touch of scorn in his tone, he stopped and bowed on bended knee. "I thought you would like your news with haste, and not with formality."

"A servant can honor his King and make haste at the same time," said King Alexandros sternly.

The man visibly bristled, but he stayed with his head bowed, "Yes, sire. You wish your report?"

"Yes," said King Alexandros.

"The Triune Halls have been taken fully, and the family housing in the city is under arrest. The students and teacher have been captured, or killed if they offered resistance." He sniggered as if this was humorous.

"And the Prince was found?"

The man's face darkened with anger, "He has made his choice, Sire. He was seen escaping into secret passageways under the Triune Halls with a band of traitors. We are searching for them now, along with a few other groups of fools like them. It will only be a matter of time."

King Alexandros fought the impulse to show relief. He turned away from the Captain, just in case his face showed something, and he stamped his stave of office on the ground next to him.

"The Fool!" he shouted. He meant himself, but he hoped the Captain would think that he meant his son. "You will bring the students and their teachers to the dungeons here in the palace, and bring their families as well."

"The dungeons will be overly full."

"So?" King Alexandros said, hoping the man assumed he wished for cruel conditions. In reality, he hoped that at least the families would be reunited for a short while before their deaths at the hands of the sorceress. It was more than he himself could hope for at this point.

"As you wish, sire," said the man, sounding almost surprised.

When King Alexandros swept his robe around to face the man again, the Captain bowed even deeper. It seemed the Drinaii only respected cruelty. "You will oversee their movement to the dungeons personally."

"My men are perfectly capable . . .

"You will do as I say, unless you wish to find yourself out of commission," said King Alexandros.

"I serve you, King, but my mistress has the right to-

"She is not here, and I am. Besides, if the prisoners escape, she will hold you responsible, no matter if your men do the work or if you do."

"True," said the Captain. "Your will is wise, O King," said the man in an oily manner.

"Get out, and send in my woman," said King Alexandros . . . "that blonde from yesterday."

The Captain smiled slowly, and nodded. "Your pleasure is admirable, sire, as your commands are wise, it will be as you wish," he said, and then he bowed all the way out of the room.

In a few minutes, a young blonde woman was thrown into the throne room, in a bustle of mussed clothing. Her face was purpled, and her eyes were full of tears, but when the door closed, she raised herself up proudly and approached King Alexandros.

Up close, he knew that the purple "bruises" were really just makeup, and her tears were probably false. She was his most useful informant, and an expert with poisons. Any of the Drinaii who came too close to her usually died. Sadly, he realized, that this female assassin was the only person he could trust in his Kingdom.

"Your pleasure, sir?" she asked in a purr.

"My son, Mina?" he asked.

"Safely away, or as safe as he can be in the underground passages between the Halls and the Sea. The allies will come for him, and for the other refugees."

"Good," he said. Then he smiled sadly at her. "You have what I need for when the sorceress arrives?"

She reached into a hidden pocket in the folds of her dress, and drew forth a red ring. "Inside," she pointed, "there is a hidden pocket filled with poison. When it touches the skin, it will kill within minutes. The antidote is-

"I will need no antidote," he said brusquely.

"I think all misunderstood Kings should have an antidote," she said softly.

"No," he said, turning away from her and gazing at the historical tapestries that hung on the left wall. He hoped that a few of his old allies would recognize his country's need. "Now I will give you your last commission."

She put her hand on his arm, and he looked at her. She looked troubled. "Last, sire?"

"Last."

She bowed her head, "As you wish, sire."

"Leave Skycliff, and go to Fraynan village in Wylandria. There, you will meet with the one armed maiden, and she will give you your next assignment." He pulled out a purse of gold, "this is half of what you will receive on completion."

"How will I be paid if you die?" she asked shrewdly.

"The one armed maiden will take care of payment," he said.

She nodded, but she still looked concerned. "You deserve better than what Kalidess will have in store for you, my King," she said softly.

"I deserve far worse for the betrayal of my people, my God, and my son," he said, feeling the weight of his sins in his guts. "I sought vengeance, and I sought to strike down anyone that opposed me. I do not know how Kalidess plans to reward me, but I know I will not be the same man, even the husk that I am. I cannot escape her," he said.

"Surely I could secret you out of the capital-

"No," he said heavily, then he pulled up his sleeve to show her something he had never shown anyone else. The mark that Kalidess had given him as contract. It looked like a twisted, fiery burn scar. "If I ran, she would make me feel it through this thing on my arm."

"It is a scar," she said, examining it.

"No, it is poison and sorcery. The only time she was truly angry with me, she sent me pain through it, and it was a fiery pain that started there and seemed to boil through my veins to my heart. I cannot withstand her."

Mina took a half step forward, and laid her tiny muscled hand on his cheek. "I will . . . think of you, dear King, and someday I will tell your son of your sacrifice," she said.

"No," King Alexandros stated firmly. "It is better that he does not mourn me, or lose his focus."

Mina tapped his cheek in a gentle rebuke and said, "A child would rather mourn a foolish father than an evil one, but he will mourn you either way. I know this to be true." She bowed once more, and said, "I will . . . pray for you, if the Lord hears the prayers of assassins, and now I must go."

"Use the papers I gave you, and flee, Mina. Thank you," he said.

She bowed once more, and then exited through a hidden side door behind one of the columns in the throne room.

He was alone again, and it was as it should be, he knew.

13 CLOSED DOORS

One of the last to leave the crystal treasure chamber, Clara looked back and watched Stelia shut the door firmly behind them. How many doors had they closed behind them now? How many lives were lost above in the city? How long would it take them to gather enough allies to rescue their families and friends?

Clara felt those worries mounting, but she put her hand on the pommel of her sword and drew it out, letting it light up the darkness around them.

"That's a nice bonus," Stelia said at her side, "a weapons that lights up the darkness, although I can see where it might be a problem too," she grumbled.

"How?"

"If you were trying to sneak up on your enemies, a glowing sword would be a bit of a giveaway," said Stelia.

"I don't think of Champions as being the type to sneak."

Stelia sighed. "No, probably not."

They followed the others down the dark tunnel in silence. Helena had been pulled into a conversation with Rhodrie and Shepherd Jordan, and Clara missed her comforting presence.

"I learned a number of non-champion behaviors as one of Kalidess's captains," said Stelia, "but I still think that occasionally a quieter approach is better."

"I know," said Clara, taking a moment to concentrate. "I think I can – there." The sword's light dimmed down, and they were walking in a shadowy glow.

"Good to know you can do that," said Stelia. "You're going to have a lot to learn about that weapon."

The tunnel seemed to grow wetter as they traveled, and the others in front started murmuring something.

In a few moments, Clara understood. She felt a breeze of salty air on her face, cool and sharp. She sighed a little and then breathed deeply. Relief filled her up. She wanted to get out from under the weight of the city above them.

The group picked up their face with the refreshing breeze wafting over them. Clara found herself smiling, and anticipating the open blue sky above.

Stelia put her hand on Clara's arm for a moment, and put her hand to her lips. "Listen," she whispered.

Clara stopped walking, and waited with Stelia, letting the footsteps of their group move away in front of them. She didn't like the growing darkness and then she heard a strange rustling sound that chilled her. It sounded like something large was slithering through the tunnel behind them, followed by a distant rumble, soft at first but building steadily.

Her pulse quickened. As Clara listened carefully to the rhythmic sound, she could tell that it was booted footsteps, marching towards them.

Stelia put her hand on Clara's hand, and made the symbol "run" with her fingers.

Clara signaled back, and they began to jog quietly forward to their group.

Stelia touched Prince William on the shoulder, and whispered something to him. His face seemed even paler than normal in the dim light and he nodded his head and made his way through the group to Shepherd Jordan. At Shepherd Jordan's signal, the group quickened their pace to a brisk walk, but not a jog for fear of tripping on the stones that now were littering the tunnel.

Stelia had pulled out her sword, and kept glancing back behind them. A hissing noise came out of the blackness, and Clara felt chilled by the sound. Stelia's amber sword just barely lit the space of dark around her arm, and glowed gently.

Clara willed her sword to give more light. It brightened the entire tunnel and revealed a monstrous sight . . . a tall snake woman with scaly arms, and slicked down hair. Her body from the chest down was all snakeskin, and Clara felt bile rise into her throat.

The creature hissed, and then rattled its tail, which it whipped forward to strike at them. Clara raised her shield, but out of the corner of her eye she saw Stelia lunge into the snake's tail and strike it with a hard cut.

The cut went deep and the snake-woman screamed in agony, stopping her advance to writhe in pain.

Stelia yanked her sword free, and said, "fight her like any opponent. Torso is our main target unless she raises weapons."

"but she's unarmed," Clara said, not wanting to get any closer to the hideous creature.

The snake woman had recovered now, and she bared fanged teeth and spit in Clara's direction. Clara raised her shield instinctively and heard a sizzling splash against her shield.

"They are never without weapons," said Stelia. She attacked as she spoke.

Clara lowered her shield in time to see the snake-woman's head severed from her neck by a powerful stroke from Stelia's crystal sword. Blood gushed out, and the creature fell with a thud.

Stelia grabbed Clara's arm, and pulled her away from the gruesome sight and towards the tunnel exit, following the group again.

"What was that? How did she get like that?" babbled Clara.

"She made a choice to bargain with Kalidess," said Stelia, "and she did not repent her ways. There are many half-creatures like that in the service of the Dark Sisterhood. The snake-women are called Naga, or Nagi as a group."

A shout came from behind them. A Drinaii scout had spotted them. Clara reached into her boot and found one of her throwing knives. She threw, and it hit him in the chest. He went down with a strangled shriek.

"Good throw," said Stelia.

Clara shook her head, and sheathed her sword so she could run faster. She had thrown without even thinking.

Thankfully the spot of daylight ahead was growing larger, and Clara began to make out the clear outlines of the tunnel entrance. She didn't know what lay outside that craggy exit, but she would rather be outside than inside.

As refugee after refugee poured out of the tunnel into the blinding brightness of day, Clara could hear the stomping of booted feet coming louder from behind. She glanced back, and her suspicions were confirmed. A unit of the King's Guard, near twenty strong, were run-marching after them.

Clara stopped by the tunnel's end, wishing she could at least step out of the cave into the fresh air and sunshine. However, holding the guardsman at the tunnel entrance made more sense, and would only take a small group of defenders.

Salene and Stelia already had their swords and shields at the ready, standing shoulder to shoulder. Clara stood between Salene and Dantor, ready to face the enemy.

"I wish I had my bow," Salene said quietly.

"Throwing knives will do nicely for a handful of them," Stelia said, putting her sword back into her scabbard and drawing two knives from the sheathes at her wrists. "Clara already took out their scout."

"Good, then we should only have nineteen more to contend with," said Dantor, drawing his own knives.

Clara quickly wiped her sword on her pants and sheathed it. She drew out a pair of knives and waited with the others.

The enemy drew nearer and nearer, finally starting to shout a battle cry and running forward. Clara threw her knives, and drew another pair, throwing them immediately. Beside her, Stelia and Dantor did the same. Six men went down, another was wounded, and then the enemy had their shields up.

They all drew their swords just before the enemy reached them. Clara had barely any time to think, she was simply slicing with her sword, and bashing with her shield.

"Form two," Dantor barked in her ear.

She knew what that meant from training, and her body responded. Clara and Salene put up their shields in front of the four of them, while Dantor and Stelia slashed outside them at their attackers. On the count of eight, Dantor and Stelia shield their group, while Clara and Salene attacked from the center. Their opponents were going down before them, and blood slicked down the edge of the Crystal Sword.

"Four," Dantor barked.

Now, all four of them fought again, as they had at the beginning, but they were tiring, and the enemy was pressing them backwards, one step at a time.

Suddenly, the sword in Clara's hands burned bright like the sun, and their enemies cursed and squinted in the light. Clara cut them down with the brilliant blade, and the others fought with her, now pressing their enemy back into the tunnel.

Slowly, the light from the sword diminished, and Clara stood blinking and gasping in the dim tunnel. Their enemy lay at their feet, all dead. Clara felt bile rise up in her mouth again, and she turned to vomit . . . but there was nowhere that wasn't covered with blood. She stumbled back, retching and swallowing back the bile.

"Take deep breaths," Stelia said, standing at her side. "Easy, now."

Clara sucked in air, standing straight, and then letting it out slowly. Then she breathed in again slowly and closed her eyes. "Oh, Lord have mercy," she murmured, and then she exhaled the rest of her breath.

Another breath and then another, and she could open her eyes again.

What kind of Champion could she be if a fight made bile rise in her throat? She stumbled sideways, and then let Salene pull her out of the tunnel and into the cold fresh air.

14 DARK SISTER

Pacing back and forth in her chamber, Kalidess felt tempted to press one of the scars along her wrists and arms, just for the pleasure of causing pain. It would bring her a small amount of power, but then one of her followers wouldn't understand the difference between a punishment and a random moment of pain. She liked causing pain, but she needed to keep her followers, especially those that were bound to her by magic.

Fortunately, they never seemed to realize that her hold over them was tenuous at best. They were so beaten down by their own problems, that they never thought of looking for a way out of the bargains they struck with her.

It was simply delicious.

Kalidess loved her work. She loved her Dark Sisterhood, and her loyal Drinaii army. They were perfect tools to oversee her work of spreading darkness.

She paused in her pacing to enjoy the view from her uppermost tower room overlooking her lands. To the North, for as many miles as she could see, the fields were worked by slaves. To the West, the Drinaii barracks and training grounds covered all the open area. To the East, the Dark Sisterhood's Keep stood dark and brooding against the blackened hills of Tormath Dar, the mountain of shadow. To the South, the sea caves along the shoreline housed her mer-army.

If only the world held such perfect order beyond her borders.

She paced to her map table, and ran her nailed fingers over the skin map of the world. Human skin produced a far softer and more pliable surface than any animal skin, but it could be fragile. She had to be careful handling this treasure. She retracted her nails, and let her fingers run over the borders.

There, in the North, Septily was nearly in her hands. The land of her foremother's enemy Champion Elar, and currently the home of that traitorous wretch Stelia would finally fall into her domain. Fracturing that land would bring it back under the power of darkness, where it belonged. She smiled, and licked her front sharp teeth with her tongue. Delicious.

A knock on her door interrupted her thoughts. "Come in."

The door opened slowly, and Maedess, her sister, crept into the room, her shoulders hunched like she expected a blow. Maedess' snarled hair screened her face from Kalidess's view and her hands were clenched around one another in front of her small frame.

"What have you done this time?" Kalidess asked between gritted teeth.

"It's not me, Kalidess, but Captain Raithan has sent a message." She hesitated, rocking back and forth on her feet. "King Alexandros ordered the attack, but his son has escaped along with a few bands of refugees. They've fled under the city, and –"

"Tell me, sister, what is the use of having the Sisterhood and an army at my disposal when they fail to meet their objectives again and again?" Kalidess turned away from her sister, and brooded over the view she had enjoyed earlier.

"Their pain is your pleasure, sister. They gladly give it for the gifts you give them," Maedess stated. Her voice quivered a little.

Kalidess stared out over the view for a few minutes, trying to tame the surge of rage she felt inside her. She wanted to strike out, but she had another use of Maedess, one that would require her loyalty. After a few moments, she walked back over the skin map, and ran her fingers north from her kingdom, past Septily, past Aerland, and to Rrysorria, and Wylandria.

"Do you remember your failure with the Wylandrians, Maedess?" she asked quietly.

Maedess dropped to her knees on the floor, and brought her hands up in a pleading gesture. "Yes, Kalidess, please . . . don't punish me further."

"It could have been a moment of triumph over three enemies. Wylandria could have blamed the Rrysorrians for their missing princes and princess, and with King Alexandros ripe for revenge, we could have managed a three way war, leaving all the players in chaos, which in turn would give us power over that whole region. I left Wylandria in your hands, and Rrysorria in the hands of Chloe."

Kalidess breathed in deeply, feeling the fire of bitterness run hot in her veins. "You both failed me, but I thought I could at least salvage my plans in Septily. Now, King Alexandros and Captain Raithan are both failing me." She pressed two fingers against separate scars on her wrist, and felt the pain go out of her to her intended victims. Their pain rebounded through the link, and she hummed in pleasure.

Then she smiled at her sister.

Maedess shivered, and bowed her head, waiting for her punishment.

"It seems I must take matters into my own hands, if I want to break Septily apart and gain power over the people. So, you, Maedess, will be given another chance to prove yourself."

Maedess looked up in surprise, her hair falling back to reveal burn scars that covered the right side of her face.

"You, Maedess, will oversee this castle and the everyday operations of our order, and I will take a century of Drinaii and a octet of the Sisterhood to Septily. Our efforts there must not fail."

"What of Chloe?"

"She will stay in the pit until I return," Kalidess growled. It was bad enough that her own sister Maedess had failed her, but Chloe had imagined herself in love with her victim. The thought disgusted her, and she curled her lips, and then spat into the fire that roared in the room's hearth.

"Yes, Kalidess, your will is the will of the Sisterhood," said Maedess obediently. She rose to her feet, and kept her chin up. "Would you like me to prepare your travel gear?"

"No, such a task is beneath the standing Mistress of Nox Ater. You will change your clothes for the naming ceremony, and I will prepare a scroll of standing orders for you. You must not deviate from them, for any reason."

"Yes, Kalidess." Maedess bowed slightly, and then hurried from the room.

Kalidess didn't like Maedess obvious happiness, but she had to trust someone with her affairs, and there were many in the Sisterhood that would treat this as an opportune moment for a power grab. Maedess was strong enough to hold them off, and loyal enough to hand back the power when Kalidess returned. Blood sisters were good for that, at least.

15 WATCH GUARD

As the early light of dawn crept across the sky, Clara went to wake Master Dantor and Master Stelia. Salene, who had sat through the last watch of the night with her, went to wake Shepherd Jordan and Prince William. They had sheltered for a night in a cave alone the sea cliffs north of Septily. Although they were all weary, it had been agreed last night that they should start traveling as early as possible to get farther away from Skycliff.

After nibbling on half ration bars for breakfast, the group was ready to go. Everyone still looked tired. Unkempt hair and the sour smell of sweat from fear still encased them, even if they had washed off some of the grime of the battle in the sea. Clara straightened her armor one more time, and felt thankful that it molded to her contours. Her practice gear would have chafed her after a battle, a walk, a sleep, and a turn taking watch.

Shepherd Jordan raised his hands for a moment above them, and then he said, "Everyone, we will continue up the trail to the nearest watchtower, and hope that the Watch Guard is ready for us. I called to them last night, and I will call them again on the trail. We need to keep silence otherwise. Do you understand, young ones?"

"Yes, Shepherd Jordan," the students said together.

Clara found herself saying it along with them, and her cheeks warmed, but Helena put her hand on Clara's arm and smiled up at her.

"Same formation as yesterday," said Master Dantor.

Clara, Salene, William, and Master Stelia knew what he meant and they took their positions with the group, spread out among the students to protect them. Clara and Stelia were still in the rear, with Helena walking just ahead of them with Rhodrie. They left the cave, and followed a dirt and sand path that led away from the sea and to the north, towards Trader's Cove, and further beyond that to Rryssoria. The air felt damp, and clouds overcast the sky overhead from horizon to horizon.

Walking with leaden legs up the trail, Clara wished they had more to eat, and more water to drink. They had decided to ration themselves, because only a handful of them carried small packs of supplies. She knew she couldn't complain, considering that all of them were probably hungry.

Shepherd Jordan led their group, whistling like an osprey, and then waiting, and then whistling again.

He didn't receive an answer, and the hours of walking went on, with little change. The trail that they followed went at a slight angle upwards almost parallel to the sea. As they progressed slightly higher on the embankment, Clara noticed that they were moving from short grass, and scrubby bushes to more bushes and a few small trees with branches that bent away from the constant wind from the ocean. When the sun had fully risen so that the clouds were brighter, although not dispersed, Clara wished for a break, and she could see the younger students visibly sagging as they walked.

A new whistle came from in front of the group, and Shepherd Jordan suddenly stopped, raising his hands in a signal to wait for the others. He whistled one more time, a short trilling sound.

A series of short, proud cries answered him from above, and an osprey swooped around a bend in the trail, and landed on Shepherd Jordan's staff, wrapping its sharp talons around the crystal, and settling its dark wings with brown tips by around its white breast.

The bird eyed Shepherd Jordan steadily with unblinking yellow eyes, and then shifted its head to survey the group. It opened its dark beak slightly, and trilled.

Shepherd Jordan answered in a short whistle, and the osprey refocused its gaze on him.

After a series of complicated whistle exchanges, the osprey beat the air with its wings and rose in flight. Shepherd Jordan watched the bird go, and then turned to them with a smile.

"I think we can take a break for a moment, and then go on. The Watch Guard will come to our aid, but we will probably have to make our way to them on foot. The tower is still guarded by them, and not by the Drinaii."

Clara felt elated by the news, and watched the bird soar around a bend in the trail ahead. She wanted to race after it, all of her previous weariness forgotten.

The others must have felt the same, for after a short rest they all stood, restless. They continued on the path past midday and into the long afternoon. Clara realized that a short flight for the osprey might mean a long walk for them.

Clara started to feel numb from muscle weariness. Her memories of the battle came in short, bloody flashes, and terrified moments of worry. She hoped her parents had made it out of Skycliff safely. She tried to push it all aside, but it was with her every step. She hoped the Watch Guard would have news of their families, of the people they had left behind. She put her hand on the pommel of her crystal sword, and felt it warm to her touch.

Finally, she could see a watchtower rising above the scrubby trees around the next bend in the trail.

Weathered stone blocks held up the tall tower, with large openings at the top. A lighthouse at night and a watchtower for fires by day, the watchtower stood as a beacon of hope and safety.

"We won't have much time to rest here," said Stelia in her gravelly voice. It was the first time she had spoken to Clara since that morning, seeming to be lost in her own thoughts.

"What do you mean?" asked Clara.

"The Drinaii will be coming to take the tower under their

command as soon as Skycliff is subdued. We may have a day, maybe two, before they come here."

Clara felt chilled and anguished by Stelia's words. "How much . . . what do the Drinaii do to 'subdue' a city?"

"They kill or imprison the defenders, the officials, anyone of importance or anyone who fights back, and then they put the whole city on orders not to move from their residences for two days. At the end of the two days, if the villagers have complied, the Drinaii allow them to begin their regular business for a few short hours a day. The time is expanded if the villagers continue to treat the Drinaii with fear and respect."

Clara thought over Stelia's words, and then of the more horrific rumors she had heard about the Drinaii. "I had heard they butchered whole cities and villages."

Stelia looked out over the edge of the trail away from her. "It depends on the importance of the place. Small villages are places for them to take out their bloodlusts, and to capture slaves, usually women and children. Cities of importance must be kept active and working, some farming communities are left to sustain the Drinaii army, but not with many men of middle age left. They leave just enough people, usually women and children, to work the land and provide for the Drinaii and the Dark Sisterhood."

"What happened . . . well, how did you become one of them? You've never told me. And how did you know my mom, before you even came to Septily?" Clara asked, knowing that she might be asking too much.

Stelia clenched her jaw. "I was 'rescued' from my village by Kalidess and raised by her until I came of age to join the Drinaii. The rest is not my story to tell."

"I'm sorry, but what if my mother can't tell her story?" Clara murmured quietly.

"She will," said Stelia, pinning Clara with a steady gaze. "Juliay's a strong woman, and your father is a clever man. If anyone can find a way out of Skycliff, they can."

Clara nodded, and looked away. She hoped Stelia was right. She trusted her judgment despite her past. Stelia had always been kind to her, even if she had shielded Clara from most of her past. Clara had known that Stelia had lived with Kalidess but not the part about being raised as her own. She wondered how anyone could handle that life, and how Stelia had escaped it. At the same time, what worried her most, was the fact that she didn't know her own mother's past, and how it intersected with Stelia's past.

She looked towards the tower again, wishing it held some the answers to her questions.

At the edge of the trail a young man stood waiting for them, with an osprey on his wrist. His white-blonde hair and light gray clothing matched his bird, and he looked as if he were assessing them with the sharp eyes of his hawk.

"Well met, Watch Guard," said Shepherd Jordan, giving the young man a respectful nod. "I am Shepherd Jordan, and with this group of refugees, I seek your aid. As you are aware, Kalidess, the Dark Sisterhood, and the Drinaii have taken Skycliff, and the King has betrayed his own people."

"Well met, Shepherd Jordan," said the young man in a musical voice. "I am Watchman Odran, and I come to welcome you to shelter and sanctuary for as long as the people of Byar's Lighthouse may offer it, which may be for a very short time. I have news to give you all, but I'm sure you would like a wash and a meal before that."

"That is most kind of you," said Shepherd Jordan. He turned and nodded to the others, and followed Odran into the clearing by the base of the lighthouse.

A huge group of people were milling around in the clearing, some of them obviously from Skycliff, while small groups of the Watch Guard stood at the edges of the clearing.

Clara swept her gaze over the group of people, looking frantically for her parents, and they were there . . . looking at her and her group.

Her father shouted exuberantly, and grabbed her mother's hand. They ran across the clearing to throw their arms around her.

Enveloped by their embrace, Clara reveled in the sound of their voices, and the smell of their clothes.

"Clara, Clara," her father murmured into her hair.

"We thought we lost you," said her mother quietly, "but I should have known you would be all right."-

"I'm so glad you escaped," said Clara, feeling tears choke her voice.

"It's all right," said her father. "All right, now that we are together." He hugged her hard, and then released her, looking over her armor. His eyes focused in on the pommel of her sword. "I'm glad you received your sword of power before the battle."

"Actually I didn't," she said. "It's a long story."

Before she could tell them the tale, Salene and Helena came up, both with tears on their faces.

"Our parents are missing," Salene said. She held Helena close to her side.

Clara knelt and threw her arms around her, holding Helena while she sobbed. Salene knelt down with them, and Clara put an arm around her too, so that they huddled protectively together.

Clara felt her father's heavy warm hand on her head.

"May the Lord protect those we love, and heal our hearts, may He give us strength for the journey ahead, and may He smite our enemies. Amen."

Clara opened her eyes and caught Salene's gaze. They were both surprised by the ferocity of her father's prayer. He usually prayed for peace, discernment and wisdom. Now he prayed for the fall of their enemies. Clara reeled from the shock of it, feeling as if numbness spread through her limbs.

She didn't have time to think over it all, as there was a shout for order above the din of greetings and conversation from the crowd. She stood up, and held Helena close to her side.

Shepherd Jordan stood next to an older Watch Guard on a large round stone by the base of the lighthouse, and held up his staff. The crystal tip glowed brighter than the light that came through the heavy gray clouds above them.

"Friends, I greet you in the name of our risen Lord, the messiah and savior of our people, Christos."

The crowd murmured, "Amen," together, and then grew silent, waiting.

"Darkness has entered Skycliff the heart of Septily, and it is our calling to dispel that darkness with light and strength. The Watch Guard will guide us to a place where we can meet with allies, and regain our strength so that we may take back the city, and our land."

Some of the crowd said, "Amen" again, but some murmured worriedly with each other.

"Do not Fear, says the Lord our God, for He is with us."

"Why has he allowed this to happen to us?" grumbled a large man a few feet away from Clara and her group.

Shepherd Jordan raised both his hands. "Why does He forgive us when we brought sin into the world? Why does he give us joy? Why does he allow illness? It is not always clear if he is testing us, or strengthening us, or being merciful to us." He paused, and then looked straight at Clara through the crowd. "This time has been coming for a long time, and we have not been clear-sighted enough to see the danger. But he has provided us with a new Champion, a Champion who will shine His light in the darkness."

"A Champion? Here? Where?" different people from all over the crowd asked the questions.

Clara felt the earnestness of Shepherd Jordan's gaze, and she knew it was time. With a rapidly beating heart, she stepped away from Helena.

Salene reached out and put her arms around the little girl.

Clara drew her sword, and held it above her head. "A light shines in the darkness, and the darkness has not overcome it," she said loud and clear. The sword blazed like the sun above her head, and people around her gasped and drew away, squinting and shielding their eyes.

"Amen," said Shepherd Jordan.

The crowd of refugees and Watch Guard murmured a second

Amen.

Clara re-sheathed the sword, and looked at Shepherd Jordan. Having the whole crowd look at her made her uncomfortable, she realized.

"We will leave to meet our allies tomorrow morning," said Shepherd Jordan. "Now, let us greet our friends, give thanks and eat."

There were murmurs of agreement and quiet conversations started all around.

"Champion?" Juliay said softly, and then wrapped Clara in a fierce embrace.

Clara just stayed there in her mom's arms, with her eyes closed. She had so many questions, but holding on to her mom seemed far more important than any of them.

16 OCEAN PATH

Down a narrow path, Stelia followed the rest of the refugees to the ocean. They were headed to the sea again, further north and away from Skycliff. The Watch Guard assured them that they would be meeting allies in Trader's Cove, and small inlet in the narrow land of Mochant, the land known for merchants and traders that paralleled the Grandan River which wound between Septily, Rrysorria, Wylandria, and parts of Aerland into the Wild Beyond. A message had been given to them by an agent that they wouldn't name, and spread to all the old allies of Septily. A part of her felt relieved to be getting further away from the Red Drinaii and the Dark Sisterhood, but a part of her wanted to just turn and fight. For years she had been in hiding in Septily, staying out of reach of the Dark Sisterhood, but now they were attacking her new home, and again, she was powerless against their greater numbers. Despair thickened inside her.

"Stelia?" Clara interrupted her thoughts, just like old times.

"Yes, child," Stelia said, wondering if Clara would take the bait. Clara had never liked being called child, even when she was one.

Clara smiled instead, and then said, "Will they follow us, or will they abandon the trail and fortify their hold on Skycliff and all of Septily?"

Stelia looked down at the sand path, strewn with sea grasses and tiny rocks. "That will depend on Kalidess's plans, although I'm sure that if we are allowed to escape here, she will be waiting for us later, depending on how far we go from Septily."

"Does she normally set traps?"

"She loves to play with her prey, once she sure she has them in her grasp. It is one of the trademarks of all the Dark Sisterhood. They enjoy inflicting pain on others." Stelia's stomach muscles clenched remembering old tortures, and the things she had done to avoid them.

Clara's blonde hair escaped slightly from her tight braid that wound its way around her head, her blue eyes were bright and determined, her brow slightly furrowed.

Another question would soon be coming, Stelia was sure. "Whatever happens, Clara, do not lost your faith in the Lord, no matter what you may eventually see, or what happens to all of us. Keep hold of the rock of salvation." This came out fiercely, and Stelia looked away again. She realized she should have been given herself that advice.

"I will," Clara said quietly. "I will hold fast."

"Good, now let's keep watch, and let the others work out the strategy for now . . .although I suppose you should be working on how to strategically defend this group in your head, for an exercise in tactics even if it comes to nothing."

"Of course," Clara said, smiling a little again.

They both fell silent, and Stelia tried to keep her thoughts clear of the nightmarish memories that flashed through her mind. She had to pay attention to the trail behind them, keep watch. She turned around and walked backward for a moment, then stopped.

Had she seen a flash in the underbrush above them? She wasn't sure.

An osprey flew up and away from the group, towards the flash she had spotted. It circled slowly, and then dove swiftly back towards them, slowly only as it neared its trainer. It let out a series of notes, and Odran stepped to the side of the trail to let the rest of the group pass him.

As Stelia neared him, he put his hand up in a signal for quiet, and she nodded.

Clara looked back at her, but Stelia waved her hand in a "go" gesture.

"There is only one of them up there," said Odran quietly.

"One of the Drinaii?" asked Stelia.

"Yes," Odran said. "There are no others and Louras has a keen eye for anything out of the ordinary," he said as he stroked the osprey's breast feathers.

"I'll take care of him," Stelia said.

"We go together," said Odran.

Stelia looked him over and realized that although he was thin and spare, he was all muscle. Although he was younger than she was, he was old enough by Watch Guard standards to be fully trained and independent. "All right," she said. Then she led him off the trail and into the tall grasses and up the steeper terrain between the switchbacks of the trail.

Stelia moved silently, and Odran followed behind her like a shadow.

Stelia led him up the hill above where they had seen the Drinaii, and then they circled back to come down above him.

The man's red leather armor stood out amongst the gray and green of the sea scrub that lined the cliffs, and he peered intently at the trail below them. He had seen them leave the trail perhaps and expected them to come at him from below.

As they neared, Stelia slowed down to a crawling pace, and drew one of her throwing knives. As she drew her arm back, Odran grabbed her wrist.

She looked at him, surprised.

He signaled her, "no kill."

Stelia frowned at him, but then nodded. She didn't like knifing a man in the back either, but it had seemed expedient. She replaced her knife, and pulled out her crystal sword. It glowed softly, but she didn't plan on using it unless it became necessary. She brought her shield up, jumped down the few feet separating them from their enemy, and then bashed him in the back of the head with her shield.

He toppled forward. Her momentum, with the shield's hardness, had knocked him out.

Ordran went forward slowly, and rolled him over with his foot.

Stelia bit back a curse. She hadn't cursed in years, but the impulse was hard to hold back at times, especially times like this one. The Drinaii was none other than Jennar, her old friend.

"You know him?" asked Ordran perceptively.

"In my past, I served the Dark Sisterhood, before the Lord called me away from that miserable existence."

"I had heard," said Ordran.

At her shocked glance, he merely shrugged. "It is the job of the Watch Guard to watch, to listen, to know, and to protect."

Stelia nodded.

"So he is?"

"An old friend and an enemy at the same time. I don't trust him."

"But we cannot leave him here, not with his knowledge of our direction."

"And killing him in cold blood is not of the Way, and I am of the Way now . . ." said Stelia.

"Good," said Ordran. "Let's bind him, gag him, and carry him down to our group. We'll get others to carry him too, and take him with us. Perhaps he can be saved . . . like you."

"I doubt it," Stelia said. "He has done atrocious things."

"and you did as well," said Ordran.

"I repented, I gave it up, and I left the order. The grief and sorrow and pain of what I've done will haunt me forever."

"No, the Lord loves you, and you are free," admonished Ordran.

Stelia breathed in and out slowly. "Yes, but the past haunts me."

"And one day there will be no more tears," said Ordran gently.

"One day," said Stelia, looking down at Jennar.

Together, they bound Jennar with a bit of cord that Ordran carried in his pack. Stelia took all of Jennar's weapons and added them to her own arsenal that she carried, all except his darts. She couldn't be too sure that they weren't poisoned. She wrapped them grimly inside of an old cleaning cloth and buried them under a rock by the side of the trail. She didn't want to accidentally brush up against them in her kit, and she didn't trust them out in the open.

Jennar was heavy, but between the two of them, he was a manageable load.

Near the end of the trail, Dantor waited for them, his mouth set in a firm line. "Did you think of telling us where you were going?" he asked, his voice tight and low.

"There were two of us, and just one of the enemy," said Ordran calmly. "Louras scouted for us to make sure."

Dantor ran his hand through his short hair. "It could have been a fatal mistake, an ambush, a –

"It was not, and as a scout I've dealt with similar situations alone with no partner," said Stelia firmly. She knew that Dantor cared for her, but she needed no babysitter.

"We are at war, and communication is essential."

Stelia took in a deep breath, thought of her own experiences in the Drinaii as an officer, and then nodded her head. "Agreed."

With a nod from Ordran, she set their prisoner down for a moment of rest. He stirred a little, and his hand strayed towards his missing weapons' belt.

"This is that Drinaii from the Hall," said Dantor. He looked at Stelia with concern.

"You think you're man enough to handle Sarya, the Storm of the Desert?" chuckled Jennar, coming slowly awake and looking at Dantor with an expression of amusement. "No man has ever-

"No man has ever been right for me," said Stelia. "Missing something, Jennar?" she asked, running her hand over his weapons' belt.

"You still know how to tempt a man," said Jennar, eyeing her lasciviously.

Stelia kicked dust in his face, and stepped back quickly.

His hand snaked out, but missed her foot by mere inches. "Still faster than me," he muttered. "So, are you all going to torture me, or kill me quick?"

"We're going to take you with us," said Dantor. "The Lord welcomes all to his Halls, in his grace."

"I don't see any Halls," Jennar muttered. "The Triune Halls have fallen to the Dark Sisterhood and the Drinaii now."

"Not for long," Dantor said quietly.

"That's why you're running away with your tail tucked between your legs?" taunted Jennar.

"We have allies, and power that you do not comprehend," stated Dantor calmly. "Have you shown him your sword, Stelia?"

"I didn't need to use it on him," she said. "The flat of my shield was too much for him." She smiled a little, and then slowly drew her crystal sword from her sheath. The glow was dim, but noticeable.

"They gave you a crystal blade?" Jennar said. His eyes opened wider, and his jaw slightly dropped.

"The Lord gifted me with armor, the kind of armor that can withstand both spiritual and physical attack," said Stelia. "It is an honor that I am unworthy of, and yet it is mine." She noticed the sword's light grew stronger as she spoke.

"You've changed," Jennar stated, his face grew tight and grim again. "I didn't understand how much until now."

Ordran held out his hands peaceably to Jennar. "That kind of change is waiting for you, Jennar. You only have to choose the Lord, repent, and you will be cleansed from all unrighteousness."

"Bah." Jennar spat in the dust at Ordran's feet.

Dantor raised his hand, as if to cuff Jennar, but then he stopped himself. "Let's get going. The others are far ahead of us now. Get on your feet, Drinaii."

Jennar stood up slowly, as if encumbered by his tied hands.

Ordran moved to help him, but Stelia put her hand on his arm. "Don't. Remember how quickly he moved to grab my foot."

Ordran nodded, and stood back.

With Stelia in the lead, Dantor next to Jennar, and Ordran trailing behind, they walked fairly quickly down the trail. Jennar didn't try to escape, which surprised Stelia, but she supposed he either hoped to gain more information, or that he was biding his time for a more opportune moment.

17 THE PRICE OF REVENGE

Down on his knees, with his neck uncomfortably exposed, King Alexandros wanted only one thing: a swift death. He knew he deserved no mercy. He knew that Kalidess had him under her power, and he could do nothing about it. What mattered most was that his son was safe from the evil that had stolen his father's heart for too long.

After the defeat of the Halls, Kalidess and eight of the other witches from the Dark Sisterhood had entered Skycliff. Dark clouds and rain came with them, and the whole land seemed to be in mourning. They had taken charge over everything in the castle, including him.

Alexandros had wanted vengeance. He had wanted power over those who had not allowed him to take vengeance. The Triune Halls had stood against him years ago, just after his dearest wife had died from Rrysorrian poison. They, and the Governors, had not backed an attack on the Rrysorria. So he had found other means. The Dark Sisterhood had been easy to contact, and Kalidess's promises were sweet to his ears. He had known that her sinister power could be terrible, but he had told himself that he could handle her. What a fool he had been. The only good thing he had done was to drive William away from the court life and all his dealings with Kalidess.

Shaking in his royal robes, down on his knees in his own throne room, he knew that he had dealt with one of the devil's own minions.

Kalidess's deals had taken a bitter turn when he had met her in secret just over two years ago and entered his formal contract with her. The scar on his arm that allowed her to give him pain was the bitterest pill of all. That he had allowed her to put it there, had craved vengeance so that he was blind to her evil . . . it ate at him now. For years he had drowned himself in wine, clinging to her promises and trying to shield himself from his own actions.

"Alexandros, Alexandros," purred Kalidess, putting her hand on his head.

"Yes, Kalidess," he said dully. He felt her fingers tense on his head, and then she twisted his short locks between her slim fingers until it felt like she was trying to yank his hair out. He gritted his teeth. "Yes, my Queen," he amended. The words were a bitter taste in his mouth.

"That's better," she said. "My Captain tells me you ordered him about, is this true?"

"Yes, my Queen," he said.

"To what ends?"

"None save my own whims, mistress" he said firmly, and then he wondered why he even bothered being polite. Possibly he could push her to kill him quickly if he became rude. He shook his head out of her grasp and stood defiantly just inches from her, looking down into her narrow dark eyes. "I am King of this land, and your men are mere servants," he sneered.

"I see," she said, tightening her jaw. She reached out and put her hand on his arm, right where she had given him her mark.

Pain burned and stabbed him, but Alexandros stood defiant. His knees felt like buckling, but he wouldn't give her the satisfaction. He wrenched his arm free, and smacked his hand down on her wrist, then twisted his ring to release the poison.

She shrieked, and backed away from him, breaking his grasp. When she was a few feet away, she sniffed the wound on her wrist, and then laughed in her high piercing voice. "You fool! You think a mere assassin's poison could harm me?" She stood quietly for a moment, and then ran her fingers over the wound in a caress. The poison poured out of the wound, and the skin closed as he watched.

It sickened him, that he could do no more than give her a harmless scratch. He could push the poisoned ring into his own skin, but he could not be sure that there would be enough.

He drew his sword, the sword of the Kings of Septily. It had shone with a dark purple when he had first received it, but the crystals on the hilt were now dark and cracked. It was still a blade with a sharp edge and that was all that mattered now. He lunged for the sorceress, but instead of backing away she came to meet him with her hand outstretched.

She grabbed the sword in her bare hand, and began to chant. Blood dripped down the blade, but it changed as it flowed from red to orange to a fiery substance like lava from the depths of the earth.

When the first tendril of the strange substance touched one of his fingers, he screamed from the burning agony. He tried to let go of the pommel, but his hand stuck to the blade, and the fiery substance flowed firmly around his hand until it encased him up to his elbow. He fell to his knees and then the floor, screaming and screaming as the pain grew with the onset of the fire.

The sorceress laughed with delight, and released the sword. "Now, you have your reward, Alexandros: the sword which will defeat our common enemies."

"No," he groaned, "no." Tears covered his face.

"Yess," she hissed, and her eyes took on a maniacal reddish gleam. "They will all die at your hand, or mine," she said. "Your precious son that you tried to hide from me, the pompous leftovers from the Triune Halls, and Stelia . . . my Stelia," she said softly, "the traitor will die a very slow death."

A rapping came from the great doors of the throne room, and Kalidess turned away from Alexandros, with a swishing of her great black cloak on the floor.

He groaned again, and tried to find a place inside himself, a place of strength to fight the pain in his hand and arm. His tears slowly stopped flowing as he took deep breaths and centered himself on the sound of his own heartbeat. His heart had once beat for Septily, his land and people, and for his son, and for the Lord, who surely could not forgive him for his countless sins.

After his heartbeat he began to notice the coolness of the floor, and then the voices of Kalidess and Captain Raithan. He didn't look at them, keeping his gaze on the whirls in the marble floor by his face.

"-by the sea, going north."

"Summon our mer-army. They will deal with them. Any word from Jennar?"

"No, but that is as we planned. He meant to be captured so that the traitor would betray herself to him."

"If it doesn't work, he will die beside her in my torture chamber."

"Yes, my Queen."

"And the prisoners in the dungeons?"

"Sickly, but alive enough for your purposes."

"Good. Their blood will power my work for some time."

"Yes, my Queen."

"Go, and patrol the streets. Take anyone not abiding by the curfew and use them for your men."

"Thank you, my Queen."

"No," groaned Alexandros.

The door clanged shut behind Raithan, and Kalidess returned to stand over him.

"Oh, little King, did you think I had forgotten your people?" She laughed. "They will serve me and my Sisters well."

"No."

"Yes, and you will have your revenge on anyone who supported the Halls, and after that, if you are still alive, we will march on the Ryssorri. I have a score to settle with them."

"You promised me I would see the faces of my wife's killers and fulfill my destiny," King Alexandros gasped. He knew she couldn't back out of one of her magical deals any more than he could. Her magic forced her hand, and should force her to keep him alive until her part of the bargain was fulfilled.

"Oh, foolish man," she snickered. "You've already seen the face of your wife's killer, and you will fulfill your destiny as my slave. I poisoned your silly wife."

King Alexandros felt his whole body consumed by rage and anger, and he managed to get to his feet. He rushed at her snarling, cutting at her with his sword encased arm.

She easily sidestepped his attack, and he stumbled to the floor.

"Now, now, we can't have outbursts like that in my court." She swept away from him and called for the Drinaii guardsmen. "Take Alexandros here, and throw him in the rooms just above the dungeons. I want him to hear his people's cries."

They roughly grabbed Alexandros' legs and dragged him from the court room, carefully avoiding the flaming sword on his arm. Alexandros felt despair sweep over him, and he gave himself over to the consuming pain.

18 DEEP WATERS

Uncomfortable with the Drinaii prisoner glaring at her, Clara fell back to the farthest rear position. As they walked down the path to the sea, she looked over the column of refugees with sadness. Despite the largeness of their group, over a hundred, there were many missing and lost. They were all connected to the Halls in some way or another, either apprentices or family members, teachers, lawgivers, and sword masters.

They were bedraggled and worn, exhausted by the terror of their flight from their homes. Clara realized that taking back Skycliff could be a long time in coming. It made her heart break to think of the people that Kalidess and the Drinaii would kill or use.

Stelia hadn't given her graphic details of Kalidess's uses for people, but Clara had heard enough about the Dark Sisterhood not to want anyone she knew to fall under their influence.

Finally, the front of the column reached the edge of the sea. Here, just a little south of the headland, the shore went from boulders to small rocks and sand. There were three ships by the shore, all older cogs, small ships with flat bottoms that easily pulled up onto the beach. They all flew brightly colored flags with the trinity symbol in the center of a bright fuschia: the symbolic flags from the Destiny Isles.

As a child, Clara had thought that the Destiny Isles sounded like a magical place. The sea itself had seemed beyond her imagination when she had been surrounded by the rock and sand of the desert. Even after years of living in Skycliff with the sea nearby, those Islands still sounded mystical.

Now, when her hope rested only on her faith and the sword that she carried, she would get to meet sailors from Destiny, and sail on one of their ships. It seemed like a combination of a dream and nightmare with Skycliff under the power of the Dark Sisterhood behind them, and unknown experiences ahead, she felt both weighed down by worry and excited about seeing the Destiniers.

She noticed that the entire group had picked up their pace at the sight of the ships, and even the more wary of the Watch Guard seemed to walk with lighter steps.

The salt of the sea and the cry of the gulls both became stronger as they neared the surf. Clara realized that in her desire to get to the ships, she had sped up and now walked beside Ordran, Dantor and their Drinaii prisoner. Stelia had gone ahead and was speaking with Prince William.

"Ready for action, little girl?" sneered the Drinaii, out of the corner of his mouth.

Clara felt repulsed by him, despite his half handsome face. Something about him radiated ugliness.

Dantor cuffed the man on the side of his head. "You don't speak."

Clara looked at her mentor in surprise. Although he was very strict, she had never seen him angry.

"Allow me to handle our prisoner, Dantor," said Ordran quietly.

"Of course," Dantor said. He fell back a pace.

Clara matched his Dantor's step, and waited for a moment. "How long do you think until we take back our Skycliff and Septily?"

Master Dantor looked up and eyed the group on the beach. "It's impossible to say."

"Do you think we have enough-

"I don't know yet, Clara," he said quietly. "We may be able to get information from this Drinaii prisoner. The Watch Guard members are skilled in their questioning."

"Good," she said, surprising even herself with her vehemence.

Dantor furrowed his brow and put his hilt of his sword. "Remember, Stelia was once one of them."

"She isn't any longer."

Dantor sighed, and then bit his lower lip, and uncharacteristic gesture for him. "When one can be turned, another may as well. It is hard to remember that, with this . . .prisoner."

Clara knew he was right. It was in the Law. Mercy and Love for enemies. She sighed. It wasn't easy following the Lord's ways.

As the refugees clumped together on the beach, sailors from each ship disembarked and approached them.

"We can take forty or so of you on each ship," said one, loudly enough to be heard over the crowd. "Separate yourselves into three groups, and we'll take you to Port City to meet with our allies."

As Shepherd Jordan, Prince William and a few of the watch-guard puzzled out the three groups, Clara watched the perimeter of the beach. She noticed that many of the watch were doing the same, but it was still something she could do. Another set of eyes might help them get away without any further losses.

In the time it took for everyone to be assigned to a ship, no Drinaii or other creatures of the Dark Sisterhood were spotted. Clara felt simple relief.

"Clara," Juliay called.

Clara nodded to her mom and waved to show that she had heard, and then walked through the milling crowd to join both of her parents, Prince William, Salene and Helena standing in one group. She noticed that Shepherd Jordan and the other younger students were going to be on a different ship, with a number of refugees from Skycliff, and a few from the Watch. They were already wading the distance to the bow of the ship, where they climbed a short rope ladder to the deck.

Ordran and Dantor were speaking in low tones over the head of the Drinaii prisoner. Clara wished she could hear what they were saying about him. Dantor looked displeased, but he shrugged once, and walked stiffly over to Clara's group.

Stelia spoke to Ordran now, and then she patted his shoulder and joined them as well.

"They'll take good care with the prisoner," Stelia said, "The Watch Guard know their business, and they understand the ways of the Trinity. He'll be given a chance to repent, and if he doesn't, they'll make him uncomfortable."

"The Triune Halls don't hold with torture," Prince William said firmly.

"Of course not," said Dantor brusquely. He sighed and adjusted his breastplate a little: a sign that he wasn't pleased with something.

"I understand how you feel, Dantor," said Stelia.

He raised his eyebrows at her, and then his lips twitched. "I doubt it."

"Excuse me, ladies and gentleman, but it's time to board," said a man from the ship. With a bright kerchief at his throat, and a tri-corner hat, he was obviously the Captain. The rest of the sailors wore kerchiefs over their heads or around their throats, but none wore hats. The Captain also had a designated rank pin on his shoulder.

"Yes, Captain Gurnsey," said Farrald. He waded to the ship with Juliay, and they climbed up the rope ladder.

Salene, William, Stelia, and Dantor followed, and Clara took the last position, noticing that the other cogs were already pushed out from the shore, and their rowers were heaving the laden vessels out into deeper waters.

As she waited her turn at the rope ladder, Clara noticed a flicker of movement by the stern of the boat. She paused, and watched for a moment, waiting to see it again. It had seemed like a large tail fin.

"Hey, lassie, time to come aboard, then," said Captain Gurnsey.

She looked up to see him beckoning her with one of his broad, calloused hands. His face was covered in a salt and pepper grizzle, but he looked fit and fighting trim. Clara guessed that if she didn't move, he would reach down and haul her aboard.

She climbed the rope ladder easily, and turned to draw it up after her and pile it neatly against the side.

"Nice work with the ropes," Captain Gurnsey stated, "spend time on a ship before?"

"No," Clara said. "I grew up in the desert, but when we first moved to Skycliff I spent a lot of time on the docks, watching the sailors at their work. Plus, as a sword apprentice, I've been given training with a number of helpful implements like rope."

"Helpful implements," he chuckled slowly, and scratched his grizzled beard. "I take it you mean anything that can be used as a weapon. Rope is mighty handy in any situation." He smiled, and patted a whip at his side. "I never use this on friends, but I find it helpful in a fight. Rope never has the same snap, but it will work in a pinch."

"It's good to be prepared," Clara noted, liking this Captain already. He seemed to be a good man to have as an ally.

"We'll compare weapons work later," promised the Captain, and then he turned away from her and bellowed across the ship, "To the sea!"

"To the sea!" echoed the two dozen voices of his crew.

Clara watched them with fascination as they worked, staying out of their way. They were all dressed in brightly colored clothes, and men and women worked together on various tasks, even rowing. All of them looked healthy, happy, and pleased with their work.

Dantor stood leaning against the rail, looking back at land. Stelia stood next to him with her hand on his forearm.

Clara noticed their closeness, and felt a pang of surprise and shock. First, Salene with her feelings for Prince William, and now Stelia and Master Dantor? She shook her head and looked out to sea, trying to ignore them. She wasn't ready for such things yet. Sure, once she had liked Salene's brother, but they were good friends and good companions. She didn't want anything more, not yet. Still, she felt something . . . jealousy? For their closeness. Her parents were arm in arm as well.

She climbed to the narrowest part of the bow, and looked straight ahead at the horizon. The dark green sea met the hazy gray clouds in a never ending line to the sea side, and only ended with the dark cliffs and rocky beach to the land side of the boat. It felt as if the clouds were closing in on them. She put her hand to the pommel of her sword and bowed her head.

"Hey, Clara," shouted Helena.

Clara pivoted to watch Helena climb up the short ladder to the forecastle.

"I think I saw a real mermaid!" Helena pulled on Clara's arm and pointed out to the open sea.

Clara didn't see anything, and then, close to the boat, a woman's head came to the surface. Clara gasped, and the woman saw her and ducked back under again.

"A mermaid?" Stelia asked quietly from behind them.

Dantor said, "A fanciful –

"No, a sign of Kalidess's minions," said Stelia darkly.

"Like the snake woman in the tunnel?" asked Clara, although she already knew with the sinking feeling in her stomach that it had to be like that. Only people changed by sorcery could take on the appearance or partial shape of a creature.

"Worse," said Stelia.

"She didn't look bad to me," said Helena. "She's really beautiful, and she has kind eyes."

"How long did you look at her, child?" asked Stelia. "They are known for pulling humans under their spell and then . . .

"Enough," said Dantor. "Let's speak to the Captain about this." He started towards Captain Gurnsey, and Clara followed him along with Stelia and Helena.

As they passed by her parents, her mom put her hand on Clara's arm. "What is it?"

"Helena saw something in the water, it –

"It's a good reason to put our minds on our sword work," answered Stelia. She leaned down and gazed intently at Helena. "I want you to promise me that you won't go looking for mermaids in the water, and if you see one, you come get me right away, or any of the Masters, or the Captain."

Helena looked out at the water, her face downcast. Then she looked back at Stelia. "I promise, Mistress Stelia."

Clara reached down and squeezed Helena's hand. "Let's work on some blade work, shall we? You need to start practicing with that new weapon of yours."

Clara's mother put her hand on Helena's shoulder now, "Why don't I come with you two, and you can tell me about your other adventures?"

Helena nodded, and Clara smiled at her mother. "Thanks, Mom. Maybe you could show her the Ferengast form with the sword and the dagger?"

Clara's father sighed. "I can see I won't be of much use here," he said. "I'll go with the others and see if any of my knowledge can help them."

19 THE CAPTAIN'S TALE

When they found Captain Gurnsey on the stern deck speaking to his first mate, Stelia took the lead. She was sure that Dantor and Clara's father, Farrald, had never seen the way that Kalidess and her Dark Sisters had twisted the natural forms of creation for their own satisfaction.

"Captain, we need to speak to you, on an urgent matter," she said. "I am Master Stelia, this is Master Dantor, and Shepherd Farrald."

"I am pleased to have so many Masters aboard my simple cog," he said, "but I think I already know the nature of your urgent business, and if you will allow me I will put some of your fears to rest."

"I doubt –

"Please, let me finish, Mistress Stelia," he said, holding up his hands. "You wish to tell me about a mermaid someone in your party has seen in the water by the ship, and did you witness this mermaid yourself?"

"No, but –

"I think we both know what Kalidess's mer-creatures look like . . .greenish skin, slimy hair, foul stench like rotten fish breath, and sharp teeth, correct?"

"So you know they're following us and you don't care?" Stelia felt outraged, and she clenched her fists. "I thought we boarded this ship to get to safety and –

"And I will take you to safety. Safety on board a ship is not something that I can command. I can hope to keep you safe, but the weather, and the creatures of the sea, both natural and unnatural, may thwart my hopes. The mermaid that one of your party saw is not green, and not foul, unless you've seen more than one . . .which I'm sure that you haven't."

Stelia barely held herself in place, wishing she could shove the Captain or get some sense into him. However, she knew he meant to finish his talk, eventually. So she pushed her fingernails into her palms and asked God to give her patience.

"Which one of you saw her?" Captain Gurnsey asked, leaning forward.

"The little girl, Helena, saw her," said Dantor. He pointed towards the forecastle where Clara and Helena were engaged in a simple footwork lesson to prepare for blade work.

The Captain nodded, and his face looked sad for a moment, then he looked out at the sea, nodded once and turned back to them. "The mermaid that Helena saw is Evalyn, my wife."

A punch to the gut, or at least an emotional one, hit Stelia hard. She closed her eyes, and tried to think past it. "Your wife . . .

"We are from the Far Isles, fishermen and pearl divers by trade. Evalyn was one of the strongest divers of the Isles when the Dark Sisterhood came to visit us. Sister Hilthin promised divers and fishermen new abilities, like being able to swim longer without taking a breath. Many from our village took the offer, and became enslaved mer-people.

Evelyn and I refused. We planned to leave our island in search of help. The night we were ready to go, Sister Hilthin came to our cottage when I was away securing the last provisions in our boat. She gave Evalyn a comb for her beautiful hair, and Evalyn accepted it reluctantly, not wanting to anger the sorceress.

When I returned, Evalyn was gasping for breath on the floor to our house, and I barely saved her by getting her into the water. We took the comb out of her hair right away, but it didn't matter. She changed, but she didn't change all the way. She is a mermaid, but not a slave of the Dark Sisters."

"So she is cursed, but not . . . evil?" asked Farrald. He rubbed his chin. "That is interesting. I had never heard . . .well, there was once, hmm." He lapsed into silence.

"We are unable to be together but we do not wish to be apart, so she follows my ship, and warns me of danger in the seas. I still may not be able to guarantee your safety from all the elements but we are a safer ship because of Evalyn."

"I'm sorry," said Stelia, not knowing what else to say. "I had never heard of the Dark Sisterhood changing anyone other than those they had bargained with for power."

"The swan princes in Wylandria . . ." said Farrald. "That's where I've heard of that sort of thing before." He nodded his head once, "you know, Captain Gurnsey, there may be a way out of Evalyn's curse."

"We've tried everything," said the Captain, his shoulders slumping.

"But you didn't have a Champion aboard with the one, true sword," said Farrald.

"Where will I find such a person or a thing?" said Gurnsey. "Champions only arise when –

"My daughter is the Champion," said Farrald. "She will help you. The sword has many powers, perhaps she can heal Evalyn."

"She hasn't even had it for very long yet," said Stelia.

"It cannot hurt to try," said Dantor.

Captain Gurnsey looked at them all with shining eyes. "A chance, a hope . . ." then he slumped again and looked out over the water. "If it doesn't work . . ."

"You should ask Evalyn," said Stelia. "Anything is possible with the Lord."

"But we've already asked Him, many times," said the Captain, not looking at them.

"Ask and you shall receive. Keep asking," said Stelia.

Captain Gurnsey scratched his beard for a moment, and then

nodded. "I'll speak to Evalyn."

20 MERMAID

When Clara learned of Evalyn's plight, she felt an ache in her chest. She knew that somehow the Lord could use her and the sword to do something. When Stelia finished speaking, she put her hand on her sword, and bowed her head for a moment.

"The Lord wills this, I know it," she said. "Take me to her."

"Gurnsey said she might not-

"She will," said Clara, brushing past Stelia, her parents and all the others. She went to the side of the ship, where Gurnsey stood next to a small rowboat that was roped and ready to be lowered over the side.

"I haven't spoken to her yet, lass," said Gurnsey.

"The Lord's hand is on me, Captain," Clara said, and then stopped. She wanted to explain more, but she couldn't. There was an awkward silence around them as the crew looked from her to the Captain. She hadn't meant it to be a contest of leadership.

"We'll speak to her together," Captain Gurnsey stated resolutely, his chin moving slightly forward.

Clara nodded. "Of course, Captain."

As the boat was lowered, the Captain didn't take his eyes off her face, and she met him stare for stare.

He hmmphed, and then climbed down the ropes to the boat, and she followed him. When she reached the bottom of the ladder, she stepped easily into the boat, careful not to set it rocking.

Captain Gurnsey took the two paddles, and started rowing them a bit away from the ship. Then he stopped.

Out of the corner of her eye, Clara saw a large fin, and then felt a splash of water on her back.

"It's all right, Evalyn," called out Gurnsey, tapping the water gently with his palm in three slow beats.

On the last tap, slim fingers reached out of the water, and caught Gurnsey's hand. Dark hair pooled on the surface, and then a beautiful woman rose from the green depths, holding Gurnsey's hand, and taking hold of the side of the rowboat. Her green eyes were deep and sad, but she smiled sweetly at Gurnsey, and looked shyly at Clara, ducking her head.

"Evalyn, this is Clara, the new Champion," said Gurnsey. "There may be a way that she . . .that the sword she carries can help you."

Evalyn looked at Clara from under a curtain of dark hair, and said something in a lilting whisper.

Clara couldn't hear the words, and she knew she had to say something, but all that came was a repeat. "The Lord's hand is in this." She drew the sword slowly out of her sheath, careful not to rock the boat, and she held it out over Evalyn.

The light from the blade swelled, defying the dark clouds above them and the deep green depths of water below them. Evalyn's form was revealed under the water, and Clara could see how the scales were creeping slowly up from her hips and over her torso. The lower scales looked older and darker, overlapping each other, while the upper ones looked bright, new and were scattered.

Clara held out the sword, and looked up to the heavens, and sang the song her father loved to sing. "Create in me a clean heart, Oh God, that I might be renewed."

Evalyn began to sing with her, her beautiful, soft voice lifting up louder and louder, until Clara's song seemed like a whisper.

The light from the sword continued to grow until it shone until Clara could only see its white light and all else was faded away. The heat from the blade traveled up her arm in an intense heat, but she held on, and continued to sing.

Evalyn's voice began to grow quieter, and the light decreased, and now Clara could hear Gurnsey's husky voice singing with them, and then voices from the ship.

As the sword faded to simple crystal, Clara blinked at the dim darkness of the dark clouds overhead. Across from her Gurnsey was reaching down into the water.

Clara leaned to counterbalance Gurnsey's movements, and Gurnsey drew Evalyn aboard the boat, hastily wrapping her in his captain's coat. Her skin looked pale and clear.

Clara looked away for a moment, until Evalyn was covered in a blanket that had rested on the bottom of the rowboat and the Captain's coat.

She looked up to see Captain Gurnsey crying into Evalyn's dark hair, and Evalyn nestled against him, her head in his chest.

Clara took the oars, and began to row them back to the boat.

"Champion, I am sorry I doubted you," said Gurnsey. His eyes were still full of tears, but he didn't wipe them away. "You will heal the lands of Aramatir, just as the prophecies have foretold."

Clara let the oars go slack in her hands. "Prophecies?"

"When darkness fills seas and lands,
A young girl born in the sands
Will bring the light of the sword
To the people of the Word.
If poisoned by doubt the sword will break,
The storm will rise, the lightning speak.
If faith is pure, the sword will remain
The Champion will save the Lord's domain.
A defender and a healer she will be
If she accepts her destiny."

Evalyn spoke the words in sing song whisper, but Clara felt as if she had shouted them into her heart. She felt warmed and then chilled, and goose bumps rose on her arms. She didn't breath for a moment, and then gasped for air, and looked out at the dark gray horizon line. She didn't want to think of the poem, or the line about poison and doubt, but it was there. Was she really meant to be the Champion?

"You healed me, Champion," said Evalyn. "I am forever in your debt for your help in my time of need. The change was taking over slowly, but you brought me back to the fullness of life."

"No," Clara said, looking at Evalyn. She had to correct her, before things got out of hand. She couldn't take credit for something that wasn't hers. "I didn't. The Lord did in His time and His way. I am merely . . .the arm that holds the sword of light."

"And we are thankful to that arm," said Captain Gurnsey.

"Please, praise the Lord, and not me," said Clara.

"There is a reason He made you Champion and not me," said Captain Gurnsey. He took the oars from her hands and slowly started rowing them back to the boat. "We all have gifts, and some seem to have greater gifts than others."

"I don't think so," said Clara quietly.

When they were back on board the ship, the crew surrounded her with praise and admiration, despite all her protests. Clara kept trying to tell them that the Lord had ordained the healing and not her, but they didn't seem to hear her or even listen. Finally, she escaped below decks to a hammock in the corner, feigning a need for sleep.

After a short while alone, she heard soft footsteps. She peeked through her lashes, and then opened them with relief. It was her father.

He came and stood beside her, holding his arms out for a hug.

She threw herself into his arms, and let him hold her tight for a space of time. She breathed in his earthy scent, felt comfort in his hands that patted her back. Finally, she let go and sat sideways on her hammock.

"It wasn't me, Dad," she said. "The Lord gave me this sword. He gave me the timing. That's all. The power to heal . . .that's His, not mine."

"I know," he said. "All good Shepherds face this dilemma at some point in their lives, when the flock wants to worship them and not the Lord. It's a strange thing." He ran his hand through his hair, and then folded his arms over his robes loosely. "You just have to keep praising the Lord, and reminding others."

"I did."

"I know, and I'm proud of you," he said. "It takes time for the message to sink in sometimes. I'm afraid that for the Champions of old, and for you, that the message may not sink in at all for some people."

Clara plucked at the rough edges of the hammock she had chosen. "I wish life were simpler."

"We all wish that at some time or another, Clara, but we need to accept, and give thanks for the Lord's provisions and grace in all circumstances. Being revered as a Champion is not as hard of a circumstance that others face."

"I know," she said, feeling guilty. She imagined how horrific life in Skycliff might become under the Dark Sisterhood's reign.

"Why don't you get some actual rest? I'll send down Salene and Helena and they can sit with you here in the hold, and keep you company. I'll make sure that I spend lots of time tonight and for the rest of the voyage telling stories that will remind them all that you're just as fallible as the next person."

"What kind of stories?"

"Oh, you know the pranks that you've pulled, maybe a few of your early foibles like the time you got lost in a canyon trying to chase a legend."

"Not that one, Dad," Clara implored.

"It's exactly the kind of story that this crew needs to hear if you want them to stop praising you and start praising the Lord."

"All right," Clara said, feeling her cheeks get warm. She had run away from home, determined to find the fanciful creatures of her favorite bedtime stories, cut her hair in a ragged clump to show her determination and brought only enough food for a midnight snack. Thankfully, she had left a trail anyone could follow. She could have starved in the desert canyon otherwise.

"Praise the Lord for His healing and let Him heal your own heart, Clara." He touched her hair gently, and then walked away, following the narrow path between hammocks and stored goods until he reached the steep staircase at the end of the hold.

Clara watched him as he went up the steps, and removed her sword belt and her armor for more comfort and rolled back into the hammock.

21 PRISON

Between the waves of pain from his sword encased hand, Alexandros thought of ways to slow down Kalidess's conquest. She may have him, but she might not conquer all of his people. Faking complete obeisance, Alexandros had been allowed out of his room to watch Kalidess run the kingdom from the throne room. He knew he had to do something, and slowly he began to plan. Kalidess finally left, to go do something foul. He forced himself fully awake, using the pain to fuel his awareness, and he crawled to Raithan's feet.

Raithan laughed at him, "What is it dog?"

"Please, let me see the dungeons," he pleaded, kissing the Drinaii's boot. "Please."

Raithan laughed, and laughed again. "Finally acting like the dog you are . . . I knew Kalidess would train you right. I suppose you're worried about your traitor son? He's not there."

"Can you be sure?" asked Alexandros hoarsely, as the pain rolled over him again.

"Very," said Raithan with a snarl. "He slaughtered my men in the tunnels, and one of Kalidess's favorite servants." He put the toe of his boot against Alexandros chin, and lifted up.

Alexandros met Raithan's cold dark eyes, and he shuddered.

"If she didn't have a use for you yet . . . well, you're head would no longer be on your shoulders," said Raithan, tilting Alexandros head back at a painful angle.

Alexandros backed away, and put his head on the ground, abasing himself to the foul Drinaii and hoping for just a few more days of sanity. He grimaced in pain as the movement disturbed his hand and arm encased in the sword's fiery metal. "I just need to see the prisoners, the traitors to my kingdom, one last time with my own eyes," he said.

Raithan sighed with pleasure. "I love it when the smart ones realize their folly of dealing with Kalidess. Your struggle against her powers is all the more sweet when you recognize the futility. The dumb ones rarely ever realize what's going to happen to them until they are at the edge of being wholly consumed."

Alexandros let Raithan gloat, and just waited, trying to look pitiful and weak, which wasn't that hard considering he hadn't been able to move much in the last few days as he dealt with the pain. He fought the sword's control over him as much as he could, but he could feel the tendrils of the strange fiery metal reaching up to his shoulder and down his side. Soon, they would solidify and send out more tendrils. He didn't want to think about what would happen when they reached his head or his heart. He groveled on the floor, keeping his head down and hoping that Raithan would acquiesce to his request while the sorceress was gone on her errand. Raithan wasn't nearly as clever as he thought he was.

"All right, sniveling dog," Raithan sneered. "You can go to the dungeons. I wish I had time to go with you and watch you snuff all their hopes, but I have too much to do here," he said, as he popped a sweet cake into his mouth, and gulped down some wine.

"Yes, sir, thank you, sir," Alexandros whimpered, and he started to stand.

Raithan kicked him in the side, knocking him to the ground again.

The pain in his arm blinded Alexandros and almost knocked him out.

"Not like that! Bow to me as you leave," Raithan said.

"Yes, my lord," said Alexandros. With all his strength, he crawled backward out of the Drinaii Captain's presence, bowing the whole time until after he had gone out the door.

In the hallway, Alexandros slowly stood to his feet, swaying for a moment with dizziness. The hall was empty, except for a few of the Drinaii, standing at the doors. They seemed amused by him. It didn't matter. All that mattered was getting to the dungeons before Kalidess returned. Thankfully his legs hadn't been affected by the dark magic yet. He walked to the stair to the dungeons, keeping his shoulders slumped in defeat in case anyone suspected him.

The halls had been stripped of their fine tapestries. He wondered if the Drinaii did not like comfort, or if Kalidess didn't want any reminders of his former reign of the country. Most of the tapestries had held the history of his reign, and his family, the crests of his nobles, and the laws of the Triune Halls. He sighed, knowing that it had all been his fault. Kalidess would never have gotten a foothold in his country without his help. He had been a fool in search of vengeance.

At the top of the dungeon steps, two Drinaii guards sat idling in chairs, and playing cards. They looked up at his approach but didn't bother to stand.

"What do you want?" the one on the right asked him.

"Raithan gave me permission to see the dungeons," he said, and then he let a tear fall down his cheek. "I want to see . . . I just need to see the people one more time before this takes over me," he indicated the fiery sword.

The guard on the left shrugged. "I see no harm in letting a defeated fool enter the dungeons," he said.

"We'll just check to make sure that Raithan wants you let out when you're done," said the other. They both smirked.

Alexandros ignored their obvious disdain for him.

After they had let him through the door, he walked down the narrow spiral steps by flickering torchlight, noticing that it seemed even darker in here than it had the last time he had visited after his wife had died. He had thought he had caught the traitor who had killed her, but he had been wrong, so wrong.

When he neared the bottom of the steps, he could hear the rumble of voices, some crying, and some moaning. He stopped for a moment, and then took a deep breath. There was no point in being scared now. He had already failed, already was being tortured, had already lost all that he had. He had nothing left to lose, and little to gain from his actions. He finished his trip into the dungeons, and was shocked at the complete darkness as he rounded the last corner of the stairway. He went back up to the last torch, and lifted it from the wall with his left hand, and then walked down.

The voices slowly stopped as he entered the main dungeon room. Each side of the room was lined with cells that were packed full of people so that there was no room to rest. A horrifying stench of blood and human waste overpowered him for a moment, and then he planted himself in the center of the room, where at least those in the front of the cells could see him.

"I have failed you, and betrayed you, my people," he said, "and I don't have much time. You have no reason to trust me, but I offer you one chance for escape." He set the torch in a holder in the center of the room, and then pulled two keys out of his pocket. "This key," he held up the larger, older one, "leads to the tunnels below the castle, and the door is here," he knelt down on the flagstones beneath the unused guard table, and found the keyhole under one of the table legs. He pushed the table away, and unlocked the trap door, lifting it up and disturbing years of dust and grime.

"Why would we go down there? Why would we trust this so called escape?" asked a deep voice from within one of the cells.

"Because this is the way my son escaped," said Alexandros.

"You hate your son, we all know that," said a woman's voice from another cell.

"No, I kept him away from me to shield him from Kalidess," he said.

"Why did you not seek the Triune Council for aid?" asked a familiar voice, in the nearest cell.

Alexandros turned and faced Lord Gray, and felt shame rise

within him. Lord Gray's white hair had once been dark. Once, he had been Alexandros' friend, but Alexandros had treated him like an enemy and had taken away his governorship. After an awkward moment, barely meeting Lord Gray's sharp eyes, he said, "I thought it was too late. She had me under her sorcery. Besides, I thought that the Triune Council had helped the Rrysorrians murder my wife."

"What? How could you think that?" voices around him rose in anger.

"Please, there isn't time," said Alexandros. "She'll know when she finds out I've come here. You need to run, now." He handed the second key to Lord Gray. "This key will unlock the cell doors. I must return, before she finds where I've gone and what I've done. I'll try to slow her search for you."

"Why?" Lord Gray asked intently, his head tilted slightly forward like a hunting hawk.

"To know when this evil consumes me that I have done at least one thing good in the last seven years," said Alexandros. "Because the people of Septily are Septily and Septily will not die if you live," he said.

"Thank you, your majesty," said Lord Gray, bowing as far as he could in the crowded dungeon.

Alexandros stood still for a moment, waves of regret washing over him. He cleared his throat awkwardly, feeling a lump there. "Do not bow, Lord Gray. I am no longer a true King, and haven't been for a long time. I hope you will forgive me, somehow." He looked around the dark cells. "Hear me all of you, if my word counts for anything, please consider Lord Gray given back all his titles, lands, and rank. Consider him the regent of Septily in hiding, until or if my son may become King." He unlocked the cell door and handed Lord Gray the keys.

"Come with us," said Lord Gray.

"I cannot," said King Alexandros. "She had marked me, and I may yet buy you time."

"Thank you, my King," said Lord Gray.

Alexandros bowed his head to Lord Gray. "Thank you." He turned and started the walk up dark stairs, leaving the torch with Lord Gray.

At the top, the guards stood when he reached the top stair, and one of them remarked, "Didn't you take a torch with you?"

"Oh," Alexandros said, putting his good hand to his head, and weaving on his feet. "I must have . . . must have forgotten it."

"Old fool," muttered the guard.

"I'll retrieve it," said the other, moving to brush past Alexandros.

"No, no," said Alexandros. He pivoted and brought his sword arm across the man's chest.

The man's sleeve lit on fire, and the molten sword clove his armor, cutting and searing him under it. He screamed. The other guard launched himself at King Alexandros, but Alexandros met his sword with his molten one, and chopped the simple steel in half. The man leapt back, and then ran for the passageway, screeching for help.

Alexandros didn't have to pretend to waver on his feet now. He could feel the sorcery moving inside him deeper and deeper.

22 AERLAND

Prince Adrian paced outside the Council Hall. His parents, his brothers, the council, and the Wing Commanders were in the thick of an argument about him, about the prophecy, about the coming war against the Drinaii. Their voices were thick with tension, and he could hear the heatedness of their arguments through the double doors.

Across from him, in the West Alcove, which had been set aside for disputed parties of noble heritage as well as ambassadors, Kryssander lounged in front of the huge fireplace, soaking up the heat. His feathers were fluffed out slightly, allowing the warmth to get closer to his skin, and, his eyes were slightly closed, and content. He had always been sure of their purpose as Wing Partners, and sure of the prophecy, even if it meant death for both of them.

The Watch Guard woman who had brought the message about the fighting in the Septily sat perched on the edge of her chair, looking tense and alert. Her tiny hawk perched on her shoulder, and nibbled at her ear gently from time to time. Almost automatically, she whispered to the bird, comforting the bird and herself every time she did so.

Prince Adrian stopped his pacing to stand in front of her. "How long has it been since the capital of Septily fell to Kalidess?"

She looked up at him, with a slow, measuring glance. "Who asks?"

He remembered that he hadn't been introduced to her, and had been sent out when the arguing had started. She probably thought he was just another member of the 12th Wing.

"Adrian Treyson, of the 12th Wing, and third Prince of Aerland, son of Hal and Gwen Treyson." He looked at her squarely as he said it, and then twisted slightly and waved his hand towards his best friend, "And this is Kryssander of the 12th Wing, son of Kylan and Krysta, and the best flyer that Aerland has ever known."

Kryssander purred deep in his chest, and cocked his head at Adrian, "don't let my brother hear you say that, but I thank you, friend." He fixed his hawk's eyes on the Watch Guard, and said, "I think we can be considered safe for the information you hold, and in fact, I think we already know what it is."

"You do?" she said, surprise registering on her face with raised eyebrows.

"We do," said Kryssander. "You've come to tell us that our old Allies need us, that the Light needs to stand against the dark, and we are called to battle forthwith, no delay, to meet either at the Isle of Destiny or in Trader's Port City."

Her eyes narrowed. "How do you know this?"

"We are who we are," said Adrian slightly smugly, and then he amended it. "I have had visions of this time in my life since I was very young. I have trained for this very moment, to be at the Champion's side in time of battle. If he is full of faith, we will prevail. If he doubts . . .well, we must see to it that he does not doubt." He said, trying to force cheer back into his voice.

"If he doubts, we die," growled Kryssander. "So we must encourage him to have faith."

"You know the prophecies, yet you say 'he' so you obviously don't know them all," said the Watch Guard woman.

"The new Champion is a woman?" said Adrian, with surprise and then relief. Then he closed his eyes and thought of his vision. It had all come in snatches throughout the years, starting with a nightmare when he was a small child. First, flying with his best friend with someone behind him, then the storm, then the burning man. Later, he had dreamed of someone shining bright with a sword in his, no, her, hands. Finally, the head Shepherd had come to his parents and told them of the prophecy about the Son of Aerland who would stand by the Champion in the Champion's greatest need."

"She's a young woman," said the Watch Guard woman.

"How young?"

"That isn't in the prophecy I've heard, just that she's young," she said.

Adrian contemplated this news, not sure what it really meant to him. He supposed that someone closer to his own age would be easier to work with, because she wouldn't expect to boss him around.

"A young woman? That sounds dangerous for you, my friend," Kryssander teased, cocking his head to one side and chuckling.

"I'm sure that it, that she, well, I don't think a Champion is going to care if I'm a prince or a Wing Partner, or anything." Adrian felt himself blushing. He had made a fool of himself over a girl just a few months ago, and Kryssander had been teasing him about finding a mate ever since.

The Watch Guard woman looked at him, with an eyebrow raised.

"I'm not very good with women," said Adrian, by way of explanation.

"Actually, I think you would be fine with the right one," said Kryssander.

"Well, when I can find one, hopefully you will too, or –

"or what?"

Thankfully they were interrupted when the double door to the throne room pushed open to reveal Adrian's brother, Ryan. Ryan's face looked flushed but triumphant, and he waved them into the council room. "They're ready for you," he said.

The Watch Guard woman went in first, followed by Kryssander and Adrian. As Adrian passed Ryan, Ryan whispered. "I think they finally listened to the council this time." He gave Adrian a sock on the shoulder, and then straightened his tunic and shouldered past him.

Adrian smiled to himself. He knew that Ryan was a bit jealous that his younger brother could go adventuring while he had to stay at home and train in leadership. Although, technically, Aerland wasn't just reigned by kings, and the kingship sometimes passed beyond family ties, their family had served as leaders for ten generations, either on the council, or in the ruling royal seat.

Adrian followed Ryan, trying to subdue any look of satisfaction, so that his parents wouldn't be further frustrated by him. The prophecy had been given to him nearly five years ago, but they had tried to find some other interpretation again and again. He didn't want to rush to his death, but he had trained for years with Kryssander, and they were ready to do something other than patrol Aerland's borders. Aerlandians were usually amenable to prophecy, accepting small bits of destiny within their free country as a matter of fact and not just faith. However, his parents didn't want him hurt. He understood that. So he kept a sober countenance even when his father gave the news.

"We, the ruling council of Aerland, and the Ruling Seat, have decided to aide Septily and all those who Champion the Lord and Light against the dark powers of the Sisterhood and the Drinaii." He looked stern, especially when he turned his gaze on Adrian. "And we, the ruling seat, Aggie and myself, do recognize the destiny that awaits our son Adrian and give him permission to enter the battle under the direction of our Wing Command."

Adrian bowed his head slightly, acknowledging the leadership of his parents and the Wing Command.

"We will fly at dawn," said 1st Wing Commander Jyssan.

23 DIRTY FINGERNAILS

The third day at sea with a crew full of admirers made Clara restless. She didn't have many places to turn where she might be treated normally. Despite all her protests and her parent's efforts at storytelling about her very normal, full of childhood foibles, past, Captain Gurnsey and many of the crew still treated her as if she were some kind of supernatural being, as if the power to heal and fight came from her and her alone.

Finally, she retreated to the cabin that the Captain had insisted she take, which she in turn shared with Salene and Stelia, insisting that they stay with her. She pulled out the tiny comb that she carried in her travel pack and unwound her knotted, messy braid. How many days had passed since she had brushed her hair?

Thinking of that soured her stomach. It had been only a week since the attack on Skycliff, since the betrayal by King Alexandros, since the fall of so many in the Triune Halls. She swallowed back bile, and felt tears come to her eyes.

She wiped the tears away and started on the lowest tangles of her hair, when someone knocked softly at the door.

"Come in," said Clara.

Evalyn, her long, dark hair waving gracefully around her shoulders, walked into the room shyly, with a tray of tea dishes.

Clara wondered where a tray of tea dishes could be kept on a small ship like this one, but she decided it might be rude to ask.

"I thought you might like some tea, Champion?" Evalyn asked, bowing her head slightly.

"Please, Evalyn, don't . . .don't treat yourself like you're less than me," said Clara firmly. She stood and took the tea tray and placed it on the table. Pouring tea into one of the cups with a sure hand, she said simply, "Sugar or cream?"

"You shouldn't . . . um, sugar," said Evalyn when she saw that Clara wouldn't be dissuaded from serving her.

"That's what I like too," said Clara, serving them both two lumps of sugar in the tiny cups of tea. Then she handed a cup to Evalyn gestured to the small bunk by the table. "Please, take a seat."

"Thank you," said Evalyn. She sipped her tea, and then looked across at Clara. "If it isn't too bold, may I ask if you need a brush or a comb for your hair? I could comb it for you if you would like me to."

"No, I mean, yes, well . . ." Clara put her cup down and picked up her tiny traveling comb. "You see, I don't have a very good comb with me, so I would love to use one of yours, but I don't want you combing this nasty mess for me. I'm just a girl with a sword and prophecy that I didn't expect. That's all."

"If you say so," said Evalyn, looking doubtful.

"Listen," said Clara, leaning forward and thinking quickly, "did you think the sorceress who cursed you had some kind of supernatural power or otherworldliness about her?"

"No, she was an evil woman!"

"Exactly," said Clara. "She was a woman that became evil. She wasn't a devil or an angel, or anything else. She was just an evil woman." She put her hand out, and rested it on Evalyn's arm. "I am just a young woman. I have trained all my life to become a sword master. I didn't know I would carry the sword of the Champion until several days ago. I didn't know that there were prophecies or visions or anything like that about me. I'm not an angel or a devil. I'm just a young woman."

Evalyn looked down at Clara's hand, and she smirked. "A young woman with dirty fingernails?"

Clara smiled. "Yes, a young woman with dirty fingernails."

"How would you like a bath?" asked Evalyn, smiling at her in return.

"That would be heavenly, but Stelia and Salene need one too."

"Of course," said Evalyn, and then she chuckled. "All this crew, and my husband, have put you on a pedestal but they have forgotten that you need a bath. . ." she started to laugh harder.

Clara wasn't sure it was that funny that she stank, but she was glad that she had finally broken the spell of awe that surrounded her. She guessed if she went down in history as the Champion Who Needed a Bath and Stank like a Wet Dog, it would be better than being treated like something out of the scrolls.

24 TRAINING

After three days of restless pacing, haunted by memories of the Dark Sisterhood and the Drinaii, Stelia launched into a vigorous training program for herself and the others. After breakfast on the main deck, she approached Captain Gurnsey and received permission to train the others in the cramped space on the stern castle deck. With only Prince William, Salene, Clara, Helena, Master Juliay, Master Dantor and herself, they fit there with only a minimum of maneuvering around the shrouds. They could run in place, do strengthening exercises and stretch as a whole group, then run mock battles between two to three people.

Stelia had never agreed with the idea of always fighting one on one in practice. That just didn't match battle conditions. For Helena, or any beginner student, she made an exception. On the first day, she showed Helena the various parts of her long knife and how to care for it and her armor. Then she set her at strengthening exercises by herself, while she ran both Clara and Salene around the deck together. With wooden practice blades provided by the Captain, they couldn't stand a chance against her. She knew that Clara could beat her easily with her crystal blade, for hers was more powerful than Stelia's amber colored one.

After she had both Clara and Salene winded, Dantor set them against Prince William while she rested and watched their form.

After a few minutes, she called out, "Halt!"

They stopped in place, as they had been trained to do, and she went to them to give corrections. Prince William wasn't keeping his guard up.

"Prince William, that tip needs to stay up, and you have to protect yourself. These two may be your friends, yes, but in the next battle you face, your enemies won't be so nice to you."

She lifted his wrist up and positioned his hand in a better position, and then she turned on the girls. "Despite how winded you are, you should have both been able to touch him by now. He's not fighting that well, and neither are you. Commit."

"Yes, Ma'am," they both said, and Clara looked chagrined. Salene, on the other hand, flushed red and let her sword point drop even farther.

Dantor noticed as well. "Clara, you're with me for the next round, and Prince William, why don't you spar with Juliay?

The others readily agreed, and Stelia gave Dantor a quick look of thanks before she pulled Salene aside. "You're not acting like yourself, Salene. What's going on?"

Salene blushed even redder. "I don't know."

"Clara's head's a mess after the whole healing incident with the crew acting like a bunch of fools around her, but I can only guess that's what's going on with you is something completely different. Something to do with Prince William?" she asked, leaning forward.

Salene backed away and looked over the side rail. "He's . . . well, he's the Prince, and we've been friends for years, but now . . .

"You like him."

"Yes," Salene whispered, looking at the planking under their feet.

"If you love him, you'll fight him all the harder in a mock bout. How else can you be sure that he can protect himself when the battle comes? We are at war, and Kalidess will not take him prisoner."

"I will fight for him," Salene said, snapping her head up and looking defiant. "That witch won't be able to touch him."

"And if you can't fight near him, or you get injured?"

"It won't happen," Salene argued, and then she sighed. "It could though, even if I don't think it would. You're right, Master Stelia. I'll not think of him that way when I'm in a bout with him."

Stelia chuckled. "Easier said than done. Let's just settle for renewed concentration and commitment in your sword work."

Salene nodded. "Yes, ma'am."

Stelia looked over the deck and saw that Dantor and Juliay had their charges well in hand. Helena was beginning to look bored with her pushups, so she said, "For now, why don't you show Helena some basic distance exercises, help her stay out of reach of her opponent."

"With practice blades or without?" asked Salene.

"Without this morning, but with this afternoon," said Stelia. She knew she was pushing Helena hard on her first days, but each day was one closer to the day of battle. When they reached port in Trader's Cove, neutral territory, and met with the allies that the Watch Guard had summoned, it could be days or weeks before they went to War with the Drinaii. They had to be ready.

After the morning session, Stelia bouted with first Juliay then Dantor, and then the three of them fought each other in a free for all. Stelia won by using every dirty fighting trick she knew, and first Juliay and then Dantor conceded.

"Thanks for the training," Juliay said, giving Stelia a short bow and a smile. She looked over at Clara, and then said to Stelia, "you've been a fine teacher for all of us, Stelia. I don't know how Farrald and I could have raised Clara to be the woman she is without you and Dantor both in her life." She swallowed, her face taking on a hard tension. "You know why my sister and I ended up in the Desert Hall, you know more of my past than Clara does, and someday, I want you to tell her, if I can't."

Stelia felt her own throat grow tight. "Juliay, you will be the one to tell her. You are her mother and –

"And if I die, and Farrald dies, we want you to tell her," said Juliay sternly, locking gazes with Stelia. Her blue eyes looked like chips of ice for a moment.

Stelia took a deep breath, and nodded. "I will, Juliay. I have always honored your wishes, and I will honor this one, if I must. I hope it does not come to that."

"I hope so too," said Juliay, then she climbed down from the stern castle, and walked over to Farrald and leaned into him.

Stelia watched her go, not sure what to do with the emotions roiling inside her. Juliay and Farrald had welcomed her into their family, like a younger sister, despite everything in her past. They had let her train their daughter, they had offered her a glimpse of what a healthy family lived like, and she could not imagine anything happening to them.

Dantor offered Stelia his hand. "Walk with me to the forecastle and see if we can signal Ordran?"

Stelia looked at his hand for a moment, and then placed her own in his. They were both sweaty and hot, but his touch was comforting. She decided to talk about something lighter than the conversation she had with Juliay. "You don't mind that fact that I beat you?"

Dantor smiled. "I can't say that I like losing to anyone, but I know you've trained harder than I ever have. You had to, to survive the Drinaii and the Dark Sisterhood."

Stelia nodded. "True." She remembered the painful punishments that she had endured the few times she had failed physical tests, or lost bouts. She squeezed his hand and let go. "Let's see what Ordran has to say about our friend, if he can say anything via flag signals."

"Stelia, I didn't mean to bring up the past but if you ever want to talk about it, I'm here," said Dantor. He put his hand on her shoulder, and rubbed a sore muscle there.

She leaned into the massage for a moment, and then pulled herself away. "I know, Dantor. Thank you." She felt as if she stood on the edge of a deep abyss with him. If she stepped over the edge, she wouldn't be able to come back to herself.

She led the way over the forecastle where the first mate ran the signal flags.

Hesten, who ran the flags, passed their message along, although he said, "Each flag isn't a word exactly. Some are, I suppose, like "agree" or "disagree," but it's not like we make sentences that often. I can spell out Ordran's name, and get the general message across. Knowing the Watch, he'll most likely send a reply by his hawk."

After the complicated signaling of flag hoisted on the halyard, a flag was raised on the one of the other cogs that simply said, 'message coming.' Soon after, Ordran's osprey flew over their ship and landed on Hesten's outstretched arm, which he had prepared with a leather gauntlet.

"Ah, there's a good bird," he said softly to the osprey and he handed her a small nut.

She chirruped at him, and then after he had unfastened the message roll on her leg, he launched her back into the air. As she flew back to Ordran, Hesten handed Stelia the message.

She unrolled the tiny bit of paper carefully, but couldn't read the coded message inside it. "Does he think we're all on the watch? How can we understand his message?"

"I studied their code once," said Dantor, holding out his hand.

Stelia handed it to him, and watched him as he perused the cramped script. He looked calm, not guarded or reserved, but she had been surprised by news that he knew Watch Guard code, and obviously Ordran knew that he did. She wondered how long it would take to truly know him, and all about his past. Then she pursed her lips. She didn't want him to know the details of her past, so why would he share his with her? Trust went both ways.

"It says that the prisoner is in good health, but not speaking. Ordran is concerned with Jennar's real mission. He isn't sure exactly what Jennar was hoping to do on his own."

"He's too valuable of a Captain for Kalidess to waste as a distraction for us," said Stelia.

"Unless she thought he would distract someone specifically," Dantor said.

Stelia ran her hand through her hair. "You mean me." She gave a short sigh. "It is possible I suppose. Jennar and I were trained together, but we spent what little off-time we had together when we were younger. When we were fully commissioned, we were in the same unit for a while until we both were promoted as Captains." She shook tugged at the ends of her hair with her right hand. "I wish . . . I wish I hadn't done the things I did to get that promotion." She felt a burning sensation in her gut as she thought of the fires, the cries for help from the inside of that village hall, the night before she received her commission. "I was a monster."

"You were Drinaii, and a captain?" said Hesten, his voice rising in pitch.

"Until I left them, and was branded a traitor. A shepherd saved me from the slow death that Kalidess devised for me. Only by the Lord's grace do I stand here."

"Oh," said Hesten, his brow furrowed.

"Forgiveness is freely given by the Lord," prompted Dantor.

"Yes, it is," said Hesten.

"Even when we're totally undeserving," said Stelia, wishing she could banish her memories.

"We're all undeserving," said Dantor.

They were all silent for a moment, and Stelia looked out to the waves in the sea. As they rolled towards the ship, the ship sliced through them. She supposed her sins were like those rolls, and the ship was like God's grace, getting to the heart of the matter, her heart.

"Well," said Hesten hesitantly, "I'm glad you're on our side of the fight now, Mistress Stelia. I saw you fighting up there with the others."

"That was just sparring, when she gets a real blade in her hand . . . well, then," said Dantor, with a wink, "you really don't want to be anywhere but on her side."

"Are all the Drinaii trained like you?" asked Hesten.

"Not all," said Stelia. "Only those who gain special attention from their masters. I was noticed by Kalidess herself when she burned my village to the ground, so I had very specialized training from her and the Dark Sisterhood, as well as the Drinaii trainers." She tried to say it lightly, but the memories of terror and pain made her tone sour, and her voice dropped at the end. "Then when I entered the Triune Halls, I received a different kind of training which has made me stronger."

"Good," Hesten said.

"Well, thank you for your time, lad. We had best get back to our apprentices, don't you think, Stelia?"

"Yes," she said, glad to get out of the painful conversation. "Thank you, Hesten."

"Anytime, Master Stelia," he said warmly.

As she turned away, Stelia felt herself beginning to smile again. Forgiveness from others, like Hesten, was such a gift. She knew it came from the Lord's spirit within the young man, but she was still amazed by it. Not everyone could accept her past or reconcile it with her present.

25 A SEA BATTLE

When she woke up on the sixth morning, Clara had a sense of foreboding. The nightmares had been thick all through the night, and the cabin had felt stuffy. She had tried to keep still, knowing that Stelia and Salene were both light sleepers. Obviously, she had fallen asleep at some point, and they had gotten up without her. The cabin was empty and their beds were made.

Slowly, Clara gathered her clothes together and dressed, even putting on her armor. As she walked towards the door, Clara heard shouts of fear outside. It felt for a moment like an eerie synchronicity to the battle that she had heard in the Triune Halls.

She burst out of the door and into a horrific scene.

A monster towered above the ship's deck. The dark green scales were mottled with bright spots of red and blue. Any creature with colors like that was probably poisonous. The sea serpent's head towered over the mast, and his teeth were longer than her sword, dripping with something that dropped to the deck and sizzled, burning the wood. Some of the sailors and passengers screamed, others brandished makeshift weapons of long oars, or long knives. Clara realized that only a small group of people were fully prepared for battle. All this she took in a moment, as she drew her sword.

The creature spat venom, and two sailors went down shrieking in pain.

The boat tilted sideways, and the serpent's tail smashed down on the deck. Over the side, there were hideous looking creatures in the water, and Clara saw that these were the kind of merpeople that Stelia worried about.

As one of the merpeople clambered onto the rail, Clara lunged and cut into his slimy dark hand. He gave a shrill cry and dropped back into the water.

This caught the sea serpent's attention, and the creature dove at her.

Clara ducked and rolled, coming up with her shield above her, and then she ran to the opposite rail, avoiding the head and going for the tail, which she might be able to reach.

In her peripheral vision she saw the serpent strike the deck, and then raise its head to strike at her again. She sidestepped one way, and then back and to the side again as it came down. Then she drove her sword towards the side of its face. The crystal sword went deep into jaw muscles on the serpent, and venom poured out over her arm. Clara screamed in pain, but held on to her sword, yanking it back and falling to the deck.

The serpent writhed and pulled back from the ship, shaking its head.

The others were fighting now, all around her, beating the merpeople off with their weapons.

With tears gushing down her face, Clara looked down at her arm, expecting to see fried flesh and an open wound. To her surprise, her arm was whole, although her sleeve was burnt away. The sword shone brightly in her hands, its light a white so clear that she could barely look at it. She raised it up, and pointed it at the serpent. "You have no power over the power of the Lord, and his weapons," she said. Light shot out of the sword, and hit the serpent.

The serpent screamed in agony, twisting and turning in the light of the blade before falling with a loud splash into the waves, apparently dead.

Shouts broke out around her, cheers of victory. Clara felt exalted for a moment, but then she looked around her. The deck beneath her steamed from the serpent's acid, and sailors and passengers alike were wounded.

The merpeople had retreated from their ship, but the other two cogs were still under attack.

"We must get to them quickly," shouted Gurnsey. "Port and forward, rowers on full."

"Aye, Captain," shouted the crew. They clambered to their stations, both at the shrouds and the oars.

Clara could see Stelia tending the two wounded sailors, and the ship's cook was tending another wounded man, a refugee who was badly burned. He looked oddly familiar, and then with a cry of shock, she realized that it was her father. She ran towards him, but her mother held her back away from reaching him.

"Clara," she said softly, holding Clara in her strong arms. "Cookie's trying to make him comfortable, but there's nothing we can do for him now. The poison has burned into him too deeply."

"But my sword, it can heal," said Clara, breaking her mother's grip and taking the last step to her father's side. She drew the sword, and held it over his burnt body, trying not to notice the fact that insides were open to the air, and sizzling from the poison.

Nothing happened. Not even the dimmest flicker.

Her father's blue eyes looked up at her, and then he let out his last breath and went still.

"No!" screamed Clara. "No! Please, no! Lord, you can't take him, not now!" She held up her sword to the sky defiantly. "You have to heal him."

"He's gone, Clara," sobbed her mother.

"No," Clara said softly one last time. Then she threw her sword down, and collapsed to the deck, weeping.

"Ready for battle!" shouted Captain Gurnsey.

His voice sounded harsh and far too near. Clara didn't want to hear it. She curled in on herself on her side.

"Clara, get up," said her mother, leaning over her.

"No!" she shouted.

"If you don't get up now, we could still all die. We need you, Clara. I need you," said her mother.

Clara knew her mother was right. The battle wasn't over. People she loved could still die, even her mother.

She stood, and her mother handed her the crystal sword. The blade was pale and nearly dull in her hands, but she gripped it firmly and nodded at her mother.

Her mother's face was tracked with tears, but she lifted her head and looked out over the sea.

The dark clouds overhead had thickened, and thunder rolled over them as the rain began pouring down.

One of the other cogs was close now, and the merpeople were turning to face the Dawn Rider and her passengers. A second serpent harassed the other cog.

Clara took a deep breath, and closed her eyes for a moment, trying to summon some kind of inner strength.

"May the Lord's glory be revealed here, and let evil die," said her mother grimly. Her sword shimmered, and seemed to lengthen. "Vengeance is the Lord's, but I pray that my hand may deal it." She ran towards the rail, and engaged the first merman to crawl onto the deck.

Clara watched for a moment, seeing her quickly kill her opponent. But as she fought, more merpeople began to climb over the side, and some of them carried sharpened sickles and deadly tipped tridents.

She ran to stand at her mother's side and soon they were joined by Dantor, Stelia, Salene, and Prince William.

Clara engaged one mer-creature after another. Some were scaly, some had multiple appendages. She cut at their appendages, and stabbed at their torsos, sometimes finding her mark, and sometimes having to defend herself. As she fought with a multi-armed creature with two scythes in its tentacles, she found herself pressed back onto the deck. The creature was lightning fast, and her blade stayed dim and silent. She fought as hard as she could, but her muscles were tiring. Every parry she made seemed to come almost a fraction too late. She had no time to riposte.

She stumbled over something behind her.

The creature swung its scythes downward towards her neck.

She brought her sword up sluggishly.

Then a green blade flipped end over end above her and slammed into the creature's body. The creature fell backwards against the rail.

Clara stood, and finished the creature with side stroke from her sword, and then retrieved Helena's long knife.

She turned, and saw Helena's pale face, looking drawn and frightened. The girl trembled.

Clara wiped the green sword on her pants, and handed it back to Helena. "You saved my life. Thank you."

"You . .it," the girl stuttered. Then she took the blade in her hands, and the green light covered her for a moment. She started breathing slowly, and her shoulders relaxed. "I couldn't let you die," she said.

"Thank you," said Clara. Then she scanned the battle around them, and saw that the mer-creatures were retreating. She didn't see the serpent in the water, and that should have relieved her but it didn't. She wasn't sure if normal weapons could kill it, or if something that aggressive would retreat.

Something rammed into the ship's side, and the ship rolled sideways.

Clara lost her balance, and tumbled towards the opposite rail.

Clinging to the rail and pinning Helena beneath her arm to make sure she didn't fall overboard, Clara felt exposed and vulnerable as the sea serpent reared its head up, and let the ship slam back into the water.

The ship roiled, and Clara kept her grip on the railing. She saw others going off into the water, saw her mother clinging to the shrouds.

Then the serpent hit them again, and her mother lost her grip, falling past Clara and Helena and over the rail behind them.

Clara screamed.

The serpent let go of the ship again, and it started to sink back into the water.

Immediately, even though the deck bucked under her feet, Clara stood up and ran towards the serpent. She launched herself off the side rail, and jumped onto the creature's neck, stopping her fall with a thrust of her sword.

Blood from the creature poured over her hands and arm. The creature flailed and shrieked, but Clara held onto her sword pommel, and tried to wrap her legs around the slippery neck. Her blade started to glow, and the creature thrashed harder. Venom dripped onto her face. The fiery pain burned deep and Clara cried out. Gripping her sword pommel tightly, she pushed away from the creature's neck with her feet.

As they entered the cold sea, Clara finally pulled her sword free, and she kicked to move towards the ship. The coolness of the water on her burns soothed her, but her fight wasn't over.

Mer-creatures surrounded her, fully in their element.

Clara fought, kicking and swiping her sword in the water, struggling to keep her head above the surface and keep them off of her. It was a losing battle for air.

Something grabbed at her feet, and she was dragged under. The water filled her mouth, and she tried to push it out, tried not to suck it in.

A blow struck her head, and she spots appeared at the edge of her vision, growing closer together.

Then there was a strange cry, the sound of huge wings, and something sharp grabbed at her shoulders, and brought her up out of the water. As her vision went black, she concentrated on one wing of the creature above her with white and gold feathers as long as her arm.

26 AERLANDIAN RESCUE

The twelfth wing had reached the battle just in time. As the others spread out to battle the serpents, Kryssander had let out a shriek as he spotted the girl leaping from one of the boats.

As he dove towards the water, Adrian felt thankful for the straps that held his legs tight to the griffin's sides, freeing him to send arrows into the creatures in the water around the girl.

Kryssander grabbed her with his claws, and with powerful wing strokes he lifted her up. Adrian leaned forward to help his friend, so he wasn't leaning against Kryssander's upward momentum. They cleared the rail of the ship that the girl had jumped from, and Kryssander gently released her onto the deck and then skimmed to a landing a few feet away.

Adrian quickly released his leg straps and leapt clear of his saddle, returning the arrow in his hands to his quiver, and putting the bow over his shoulder. He ran to the girl's side, and saw that she had passed out. Making sure of her breath and pulse with a quick touch of his fingers on her neck, he found himself gazing at her face. A terrible poison burn marred half of her face. Underneath that she had beautiful sweeping cheekbones, and long blonde lashes. Her lips were slightly parted, and he felt a sudden urge to kiss her.

He swallowed and sat back, removing his hand from the soft skin of her neck. He forced himself to look at her wounds and start assessing the damage on her sword arm. Despite the horrific burns, she clutched the pommel of her sword tightly.

A young girl ran towards the young woman on the deck, and leaned over her. "Clara, Clara, are you all right?" She drew a green blade out of a short sheathe, and placed it against Clara's chest. It glowed, and the young woman moaned slightly.

Adrian looked past the young woman's beauty and her burns and realized she was holding tightly to a sword of power. But it was a dull opaque color, without brilliance. It wasn't the dull gray of someone who had lost complete faith, but it wasn't live either. "Who is she?" he asked the little girl.

"Clara," she said, "she's my friend, she's . . . the Champion. She can't die!"

"The Champion?" asked Adrian. He wondered how a Champion could have such a dull sword, so beautiful, and so wounded at the same time. He put his hand over her sword hand, and felt a dull warmth. The blade was dim but still live. The Champion must have some deep seated faith still inside her. He let out a sigh of relief, and then thought of the prophecy and tension boiled up in him again. This girl, this young woman near his own age was the Champion he was fated to protect, and if she doubted, he could die. If she doubted, the darkness could win.

"She can't die," repeated the little girl, sobbing.

"Try your healing touch on that wound on her head," said Adrian. He touched the pendant on the chain that hung from his neck. The crystal inside was clear and bright, like the color of a Champion's sword. The Champion's blade brightened for a moment, as if in response to him, and Clara mumbled something, and her hand tightened on the pommel of her sword until her knuckles turned white.

"It's all right," said Adrian in a soothing tone of voice, squeezing her hand gently.

Her fingers relaxed slightly under his, but she kept a hold on her sword.

The little girl looked at him curiously. "Who are you, anyway?"

she asked.

"Adrian of the 12th Wing, Griffin Partner," he said simply, leaving out his rank and title.

Kryssander had crept up by the girl, and Adrian didn't think she noticed for she startled when he spoke.

"And I am Kryssander," he said.

The girl squeaked, and turned quickly, holding up her green blade, as if she would stand against the griffin.

"Kryssander pulled Clara out of the water," said Adrian, "we're here to protect her."

The girl nodded once, and then said in a trembling voice. "I am too."

"Good," said Adrian, fighting the smile that rose to his lips. He imagined that someone so young wouldn't have been gifted with a blade of power, and a set of armor that mirrored the Champion's own if she wasn't a formidable ally.

Reluctantly he let go of Clara's hand, and stood, looking over the rail at the deceptively empty looking waters near the boat. "I'll stand watch over her with Kryssander while you tend her wounds."

Beyond the ship they were on, Adrian could see the other flyers of the 12th Wing, circling the other two ships, and driving off the remaining attackers. The serpents were all gone, or at least not able to be seen above the sea, and the mer-creatures were all swimming away, harried by the 12th Wing. He knew he should report, but he could get away with waiting for someone to come to him. As a prince, he could pull rank every once in a while and get away with it.

A warrior woman with a glowing amber sword ran across the deck toward them, "Clara!" she cried and she threw herself down next to Clara and the little girl. She looked at him fiercely and gave Kryssander and odd look, but then she bowed her head over Clara and ignored them. "Please, please," she pleaded.

Adrian bowed his head to add his own wordless prayer.

27 SLOW HEALING

Despite the awesome presence of the white and gold griffin, Stelia stayed by Clara's side as a healer from the Watch Guard and Helena tended her on the deck of the ship. Clara stayed unconscious, and her face and arm were badly burned. Stelia didn't touch her, not wanting to hurt her more, but she hovered over her, just outside the healer's range of movement.

"Get me some fresh water, now!" he snapped, looking wildly around him. He pointed at Stelia. "You, get it from the stores."

Stelia nodded, and leapt to her feet, heading blindly across the deck to the cook's cabin where the fresh water stood in casks. She helped herself to a bucket and a few clean cloths she found in one of the drawers.

Back on the deck, the group around Clara had grown. It seemed like most of the passengers and crew pressed around the healer and Clara. The griffin and his rider formed a protective half-circle, but the other side kept pressing in.

"Is the Champion going to live?" murmured someone.

"Yes," Stelia snapped. "She will live. That's what Champions do." She carefully handed the water to the healer, and then turned to face the crowd. "If you aren't a family member, her mentor, or a very close friend, step back and let the healer do his job!"

She put her hand on her sword, almost wanting to draw it.

The crowd backed away a bit, with the exception of Prince

William and Salene who pushed their way through.

"Where's Dantor?" Stelia asked them, scanning the crowd.

"He's injured too," said Prince William quietly. "The healer gave some herbs to Cookie, and he's resting over there, by the main mast." He gestured with his hands.

Stelia took a step towards Dantor, and then stopped and looked at Clara. The girl was still out cold.

"We will look over her," said the griffin rider. "I think Kryssander and I can hold off anyone on this ship."

Stelia gave the young man a quick assessment. Whipcord thin, of a shorter than average height with tanned features, carrying a bandolier of knives, and a recurve bow, he seemed fit and able enough to hold off most of the crew members individually. She doubted his ability to stand against her, but then he wouldn't have to, and if he did, he'd have his griffin by his side.

The magnificent golden white creature had long, sharp talons, a dangerous looking beak, and was the size of a draft horse. It held its wings carefully up against its body, but Stelia remembered the sight of them unfurled, and she wondered for a moment just how he would mount the skies from the deck. It didn't seem like there could be enough room for him.

If the two of them hadn't been on their side, fighting off one of the sea serpents, and rescuing Clara, they might not have won the battle. They seemed earnest about protecting Clara, and so, she nodded curtly and introduced herself. "Stelia, Master Swordswoman and Scout of the Triune Halls of Septily." She held out her hand.

The boy, she lowered her age estimate of him when he relaxed, took her hand in his own, meeting callouses with callouses. "Adrian, Griffin Flyer and Scout from the twelfth wing of Aerland."

"And I am Kryssander," said the griffin in a low raspy voice, his intense large eyes watching her carefully.

Stelia felt her throat grow dry, and she almost let go of her handshake. "It is nice to meet you, Kryssander of Aerland, and Adrian."

"Well met, indeed," said Prince William. "Your coming was providential for us." Then he looked over at Stelia and put his hand on her shoulder, "We'll all look after Clara."

"Thank you," she said, letting go of Adrian's hand, and taking one last look at Clara.

The healer was trying to tug the sword out of Clara's hands, but she moaned and seemed to grip it even harder.

"Don't try to take it from her," said Stelia.

"I can't heal her hands if I can't get it free," said the healer, with frustration.

"It has healing properties when it glows," said Helena, kneeling by Clara's side now and putting her hand on the healer's arm.

"But it's not glowing now," said Salene.

Stelia looked at the sword closely and was shocked at how dull and lifeless it seemed, almost an opaque and dull crystal now.

They were all silent for a few moments.

The healer turned to look up at them all. "I'll do the best I can to heal her and make her comfortable. We'll need to move her to her cabin, and you," he looked at the griffin," won't fit there."

"I'll stand watch at the door," said Kryssander with dignity.

"I'll see to Dantor now," said Stelia, "unless you need me."

"You need to see him," said Salene. "If Clara wakes, I'll tell her that you looked over her."

"Thanks," said Stelia. She patted Salene's arm, and then strode across the deck to where Dantor looked to be arguing with Cookie.

"I won't drink any more of that vile stuff," he said. "I can't understand how that's going to heal my leg anyway." He held Cookie's wrist, keeping a mug of liquid away from him.

"Healer Wenden said that this should take the worry of infection away," argued the cook patiently.

"Dantor, please, you don't want to risk infection," said Stelia, coming to sit by him. She put her hand to the side of his face, and ran her fingers down his cheek. "I've seen men die from infected battle wounds. I won't let you die like that." She took the mug from

Cookie, and pressed it into his hands. "Drink up, and be thankful you're alive."

He took the mug reluctantly, and then said, "Is Clara all right? I couldn't believe that she tackled that serpent. She looked badly burned when that griffin brought her on board."

"She's alive, and I won't tell you anymore until you've taken your medicine," she said.

He drank obediently, forcing it down in a huge gulp. He grimaced, and shuddered slightly. "Awful. I don't understand why medicine has to be that way."

"Emergency stores haven't been sweetened," said the Cook. He took the mug, and patted Stelia on the back. He's bound up well enough now, if you're going to look after him, I'll be getting to some of the others."

"Thank you," Stelia said. Out of the corner of her eyes she could see him leave, but she kept her attention focused on Dantor.

"So, Clara and the others? How are they?" he asked impatiently, trying to sit up farther, and then wincing as his leg moved on the deck.

Stelia maneuvered so that she sat behind him, and then propped him up against her shoulder, "better?"

"Yes," he said, "I don't like lying flat on my back after a battle. I –

"need to see the action around you. I understand," she said. She pointed to where the healer was putting Clara onto a stretcher. "The apprentices are all alive, thanks to our new Aerlandian friends. That griffin plucked Clara out of the water and saved her life." She paused for a moment, not sure how to tell him about the sword. Then she realized he might understand the crystal's properties and decided to put it first. "Clara's sword isn't glowing anymore. It looks lifeless."

Dantor closed his eyes, and frowned. He sighed once, and then said slowly, "When a crystal sword is dull, it means that the wielder has lost her, or his, faith. Her parents are both gone; she saw it happen, as did I. She may be angry, or just heartbroken." He sighed again, and his shoulders slumped slightly.

"Then why isn't she letting the sword go? The healer can't get it out of her hands. Doesn't that mean something?"

Dantor opened his eyes, and sat up slightly. "She isn't letting go? That's good. It means that there's a chance she can heal from this, and regain her faith."

Stelia didn't respond, looking out over the rail of the boat into the horizon. "It can take a long time to heal," she said.

"We can't rely on her for the coming battle," said Dantor. "Or at least not make our plans around having a Champion."

"And the battle is coming to us. We won't be able to choose the time and place if Kalidess plans to kill us before we reach Trader's Island."

"She didn't know we had a Champion," said Dantor.

"or Aerlandian allies," said Stelia.

"There is only one Wing of Aerlandians?"

"The Twelfth," said Stelia, "and these two seemed taken over completely with the need to protect Clara . . . almost as if . . . they knew something about her."

"The Aerlandian love to study the prophecies," said Dantor, "much like the Watch Guard." He leaned back against Stelia again, letting his head fall onto her shoulder. "I think that brew I drank is making me sleepy."

"Sounds like any pain herbal I've ever had," she said. She looked down at him, and found herself falling into the depths of his eyes. She took a shallow breath.

His lips parted slowly and he reached up with his hand to touch her hair that had fallen in disarray around her shoulders. "Watch over me, my Sarya," he said.

"I will," she said gently, and then she leaned down, and brushed his lips softly with hers.

His hand fell away from her hair, and as she opened her eyes, she could see that he had succumbed to the effects of the medicine and was asleep.

28 NIGHTMARES AND BITTERNESS

Suffocating darkness wrapped around her. Voices whispered slower, then faster. She didn't have enough air, not enough to breathe. Liquid poured into her mouth, and the darkness became black water with hands and tentacles grabbing her from all directions.

A white light broke the darkness. A golden white wing buffeted her face. Talons pulled on her shoulders, tugging her out of the grasp of the darkness, but then she fell dizzy, back into the suffocating blackness.

She didn't know how many times the sequence repeated before she realized that it must be a nightmare. But it seemed so real. This last time she dropped, she dropped into a kind of dimness. The voices around her were gentle, and most were familiar. One of the voices, a light tenor seemed different somehow, and she wanted to open her eyes to see him, whoever he was. But the effort took too much strength, and she fell back into the darkness again.

This time, the nightmare was familiar. She was on the ground, in the mud, and rain poured over her. Dark clouds pressed down, and she could barely make out the pommel of her sword. She gripped it fiercely, wishing it could give her some answers to her questions. Then she noticed that the blade, just beyond the pommel was broken, shorn by something greater in power. She looked up, and a man holding a sword that looked like liquid fire, stood above her. He raised his blade above her, and she bowed her head. She deserved to die.

A shriek rent the air, and a huge shape dove from the sky.

Clara looked in time to see the fiery sword plunge into the griffin's chest.

She screamed, and the world went black again. She returned to the storm, the broken blade, lightning crackled above the man this time, she noticed, but the griffin still dove, and still died.

She couldn't seem to stop it, over and over again it played in her mind. No matter what she told herself as she screamed, she dreamed it nearly the same every time. Every time her sword was broken. Every time she knelt in the mud, helpless to save herself or the griffin.

Finally, the dimness rose around her, and she tried to cry out for help. All that came out was a dry, rasping sound, a whimper. Her eyelids fluttered. She was in a dimly lit room. She struggled to keep her eyes opened, but failed. One side of her face felt closed in, and she guessed that it was wrapped in a bandage.

The tenor voice spoke softly, "It's all right, Clara. You are safe."

"Who?" she managed to say huskily, her throat burned with the effort.

"Adrian of the Aerland, at your service, my dear lady," the voice said.

She could hear a chair creak slightly, and a soft footstep. A warm hand touched the unbandaged side of her face, and she blinked again, finally opening her uncovered eye in time to see a handsome young man leaning over her, his face just inches from her own. She felt a sudden flutter in her chest, and a tightening in her gut. She swallowed and couldn't think of what to say.

He smiled slightly, and ran his thumb against her chin before drawing away. "Thank the Lord you're awake." He busied himself at a side table, pouring water from a pitcher into a glass.

"The Lord . . ." Clara closed her eyes, and willed herself to find that blaze of hope and peace she felt when she thought of her Lord and Savior. She felt nothing other than a hollow emptiness. "The

Lord has abandoned me."

"No," he said firmly. "He has not." He brought her the glass, and sat on the edge of the bed. "Here, water will help with your healing."

Clara put her hands by her sides and tried to sit up, but her right arm was stiff and painful inside a huge bundle of bandages, and her left arm felt weak and exhausted like the rest of her.

"It's all right, I'll help," Adrian offered, moving to sit alongside her. He wrapped his free arm around her shoulders, and lifted her up to lean against his chest, then held the water glass to her lips.

Clara wanted to move away from him but she took the glass in her hands. "I can at least drink by myself," she growled, angry at being so helpless.

"I understand," he said. "We've all be helping you drink and eat for the last week, but now that you're up, you're ready to take on those necessities at least."

"Who's we, and where am I?" demanded Clara.

"We're on Captain Gurnsey's sturdy cog ship, and your friends and I have been caring for you." His breath tickled her ear when he spoke, and she could feel every one of his hard muscles along her back. He was only wearing a tunic, and she was wearing only a thin shift.

Thinking of this, Clara attempted to pull away from him again and sit up, but she was too weak. "Listen, maybe you've been caring for me for the last week, but I don't know you," said Clara. She didn't turn to look at him when she spoke, because she didn't want to think about how close his face was to hers.

He let out a soft chuckle. Clara tried not to let herself enjoy the sound.

"I'm the second Prince of Aerland, fated by the prophecies to stand by the Champion in her first battle against the leader of darkness."

"Well, you're a bit late then, aren't you?" said Clara. "Where were you in the battle at Skycliff?"

"We didn't know the exact time or date, or Kryssander and I

would have been there," he said. "Do you remember Kryssander pulling you out of the sea?"

"The white and gold griffin?" Clara asked, remembering the beautiful wings. "You know him? He's . . . yours?"

"No more than I am his. We are partners, flyers in the 12th Wing of Aerland."

"But you said you were a prince?" Clara felt even more uncomfortable now. What was a prince doing caring for an injured girl?

"The third prince, the one that doesn't have to train for pomp and circumstance," he said lightly. Then he said quietly, "but I did have to train for destiny of a different sort."

"Destiny isn't supposed to be like this," Clara said quietly. She knew she sounded whiny, but when she thought of destiny she thought of the battle at Skycliff, the hurried escape through the old city, the sword of power, and then losing her parents, first her father and then her mother. She wondered who else had been lost, and suddenly she didn't want to just wonder. "What happened after I went in the water? Did anyone else die? Are Salene and Prince William all right? Are Helena and the other children okay?"

"They are all safe, he reassured her. "After Kryssander and I rescued you, the 12th Wing helped the allied forces push back the serpents and the mer-people attack. Your advisor . . . Master Dantor was injured, but he hasn't let the healers keep him down."

"Good," Clara said, smiling at the thought of healers trying to keep Master Dantor still for more than few hours." She took another gulp of water, and then put it into his hands. "I would like to try to sit on my own now."

"All right," he said, placing the glass on the nearby table. He eased her away from him, put his hands under her arms, and helped her sit back against the wall of the ship by the head of the bed.

"Thank you," she said, pulling the covers up a little higher over the skimpy shift. "How long have I been out?"

He looked away from her, and then took a deep breath.

She could tell she wasn't going to like his news.

"It's been a sevenday. The Allied Council decided to send the Allied Forces to Septily and mount an attack on Kalidess' forces in the hopes to take back Skycliff, your capital city."

"A sevenday . . ." Clara took a deep breath and let it out, trying to keep her disorientation at bay. How could she have lost a week asleep in her nightmares, and where was her sword? She needed to be up and training if she were going to be part of an attack. "Why didn't someone wake me, and where is my sword?" She threw her bedcovers off, completely forgetting her earlier feelings of modesty. She swung her bare legs over the side of the bed opposite to him, and when she looked down she saw it.

Her sword lay by the bed, obviously dropped. The vibrant brightness was gone. Dull opaqueness ran the length of the blade and a small crack marred the tip, running down towards the hilt. "No," she moaned. "Blades of power don't break, don't dull unless . . . unless their owners lose their faith . . ." she felt the emptiness inside her fill with pain.

"You only just dropped it this morning," Adrian said, coming around to the end of the bed. "In fact, it was glowing softly until that last set of nightmares you had."

"They're all the same," Clara said. "Nightmares about the sea battle, and the other one . . . where my sword is . . . and the griffin . . . Kryssander." She didn't want to look at Adrian, and definitely didn't want to tell him the details of her dream. "Kryssander is all right, isn't he?"

"Yes," he said, looking concerned. "What did you see in your vision?"

"It's not a vision. It's just a nightmare. That's all," she said, reassuring herself, and trying to avoid his eyes. "Could you find someone to get me a wash basin, and could you give me some privacy? I'm going to get up. I need to find Master Dantor and Stelia, and see where they want me during the battle."

"They've already gone," he said quietly.

"What do you mean?" she asked him and this time she looked at him directly and he wouldn't meet her gaze.

"The Allied Forces left this morning, hours ago. Only a handful of us stayed behind: Helena and Rhodrie were seen as too young, Captain Gurnsey, his wife and a handful of his crew stayed back, and those who were injured or caring for the injured."

Clara felt a new sense of loss. Being left behind didn't fit with her idea of being a Champion. It didn't fit her idea of princeliness either. "Why are you here?"

"To fulfill my destiny, Champion," he said. "I go to battle when you go, and not before." This time he looked at her fully, and then knelt on the floor of the cabin and held out his hands palms up towards her. "I give my oath, as promised years ago in the Hall of Wisdom that I shall stand by your side or fall by it, as the Lord wills, in the battle against the forces of darkness."

"You've been training to fight next to me your whole life?" Clara couldn't believe what she was hearing, and had some doubts about the sanity of his society. "What if a Champion hadn't shown up in our generation?"

"My visions were clear," he said, and then he chuckled. "Well, I guess not that clear. I didn't see you in them, just a rough figure with the Sword of Truth. I certainly didn't know that my Champion would be a beautiful young woman." He blushed slightly, and then stood up quickly.

Clara felt her own cheeks grow warm, and she fought the urge to grab the bedcovers again. "I'm a smelly, young woman who needs her armor, and some clothes."

"You said it first," he said, and then winked at her, and exited the room quickly.

Clara scowled after him, and then reached down with her left hand to pick up the Sword of Truth. The blade felt heavy in her hands, dead and lifeless, much like she felt inside. She closed her eyes, and tried to pray, but couldn't even seem to think the words. She pressed her lips together. Her friends needed her. Her country needed her. She had to get up, and she had to fight, which meant that she had to pray, for the sword would remain lifeless otherwise.

29 BURNING MAN

The smell of burning hair roused Alexandros from his fitful slumber. Waves of pain shot through him, and he sobbed hot tears down his cheeks. They landed on the floor with a sizzling hiss, and evaporated. His clothes were burned off to his waist, the upper part of his torso was wrapped in the sorcerous fire that encased his arm and gave strength to the sword. The agony was beyond anything he had experienced before. Slow, shuddering breaths brought smoky air into his lungs. Everything felt unbearably hot. And yet, he lived. Somehow, when he should have burned to his bones, he lived.

The door to his cell banged open, and a burly Drinaii walked into the room, with his sword drawn.

Alexandros hoped the man would end his pain. He tried to get up, but only managed to roll onto his face.

Hissing laughter met his struggles. He could see Kalidess's pointy shoes, the train of her dark red skirts sweeping across the floor. They stopped in front of him.

"Finally, you give me your obeisance," she said.

He focused on breathing, and then tried to stop.

She kicked him in the side, unharmed by the flames that licked his torso.

He sucked in a gasp of air involuntarily.

"Oh, don't you just love the wonders of magic?" she said to him. "It can consume without consuming, it can hurt without killing, it can bring a proud King to his knees." She laughed again. "Soon, your reward is going to be complete, dear Alexandros, and then we will join my armies in a rout of this pitiful kingdom. We shall banish all those who pledge their allegiance to the Triune Council, and any who try to work against the Dark Sisterhood will be made useful."

Alexandros groaned.

"What's that? You want to tell me that the prisoners you set free will rise up against me, and overthrow my hold on your kingdom." She bent down and patted the edge of the flames on his face. "What a good little King you are." She looked him straight in the eye. "Don't you worry about those people. They'll get their reward, just like you." She smiled, and made a gesture with her hand.

The pain intensified, and he cried out, and then blackness overtook him.

"Pity, ordinary men are just not strong enough to be my playthings," Kalidess said, frowning at Alexandros. "But he will serve me soon, and then, when this kingdom is fully in my power, I will have time for pleasurable pursuits with other more extraordinary men," she said, tilted her head at the Drinaii prison guard.

The man blanched, and swallowed.

Kalidess ran her hand along his forearm, and he flinched.

She felt amusement bubble up inside her at his discomfort, and she smiled at him showing her sharp teeth. "What's your name again?"

He hesitated and looked down. "Garson, my lady."

"Garsson," she said hissing softly over his name. "I'll remember your name."

He bowed, and she swept past him, chuckling.

30 PRAYERS

After several minutes of failed attempts at old prayers, Clara forced herself to pace the small cabin. She walked slowly over to a tiny porthole and peered out at a narrow section of deck, the rail, and the sea . . .all shadowed by dark clouds. The poison of the sea serpent still seemed to be in her system. She felt weak and lethargic, and suddenly angry. The anger filled her with some energy but not enough. She had to get her strength back. She had to help her people. That's what Champions did. That's what she would do.

Even if the power from the sword was gone, and God didn't care about her anymore, she would be a Champion to her friends and her people.

The door creaked and hasty footsteps crossed the room. It had to be him again. She didn't want him here, and yet she found herself turning to look up at him, as he reached out and put his hand on her shoulder.

"I've brought everything you need to get dressed for battle, but I have to ask, have you prayed?"

She pulled away from him and swayed on her feet, "No."

He stood silently behind her.

His silence unnerved her, and his belief in his visions and prophecies fed her anger until she suddenly snapped. "I failed. God doesn't care anymore, and Septily is under the control of the Dark Sisterhood. I don't understand why . . . why God chose me, if he didn't want me. Prayer doesn't work."

"How can you be certain that the Lord doesn't care?" he asked.

"The sword doesn't shine. It doesn't heal. My parents are dead. Septily is lost. It's obvious that God doesn't care for me or any of us."

"Sometimes we don't see the big picture that God sees. Why haven't you talked to Him?"

"Why bother?" Clara glared at the wooden wall across from her, and didn't look up at him. Shame welled up in her for saying the words out loud.

"How can He help you, if you don't give Him a chance?"

"He won't."

"Just try Him."

"I've tried. Why try again?"

"Because we need you, and you need Him." He put his hand on her shoulder again. "Please, Clara."

Clara closed her eyes, willing herself not to care. willing him to go away. Yet she found herself clutching at his hand on her shoulder. "All right, I'll try." She opened her eyes and looked at him. "But I doubt He'll answer."

"Give him your heart, and wait for his answer." Adrian kissed her hand, and then walked to the door. "I'll be back in a little while."

"Thank you," she said, although she wasn't sure she should be thanking him for empty advice. His faith was sweet, but it wasn't hers anymore.

However, she had said she would try. She bowed her head, and then felt like somehow that wasn't enough. She knelt down, and turned to face to face the bed, burying her face in the covers. "Lord, I don't understand. I'm so angry at you. I hate that you let my parents die. I hate that you let Septily fall under Kalidess. I hate failing. I hate me. I hate . . .everything. I don't think you're even real anymore." Sobs tore at her throat as she said the last part, and she fell down to the floor and sobbed onto the planks. Then she sat up, and raised her hands to the ceiling. "If you are real, then show me."

An overwhelming brightness came over her, and Clara covered her head with her arms, and bowed down. She expected wrath over her outbursts. She had read of such things in the scriptures. Instead, she felt overpowered by love, as if she were wrapped in a giant embrace of warmth and gentleness. Forgiveness poured into her, and she pressed her face against the floor and wept. She was so unworthy. So wrong in her thoughts. She didn't deserve forgiveness, and yet it was there, insistent against her hardened heart, and she let the Lord back in. She cried until the tears disappeared. When her cheeks were dry, she sat up, and opened her eyes carefully. The light blazed all around her, but she could see without pain. A figure, dressed in a white robe, held out his scarred hands to her. "I am real, Champion Clara, and I love you. Your doubts will have their consequences, but know that I love you."

"Thank you, Lord," she said. She stood up, and felt surprised by the energy that coursed through her. The figure receded and the light dimmed, until just a few rays entered by the window. She pulled off her bandages, first from her right arm, and then from her face. Clean, healed scars ran the length of her arm, but as she flexed it, she felt strong. She put her hand to her face and felt a small line running down her right cheek.

By her feet, the Sword of Truth glowed, and when she picked up it up, the brightness overwhelmed her, but she held it steady. When it dimmed slightly, she noticed with some dismay that the crack still ran down its length. A shiver ran through her at the sight of it, but she knew that she had been healed for a reason. She was meant to fight in the upcoming battle.

Quickly, she used the small basin of warm water and the cloths to at least get some of the stink of sickness off of herself. She dressed in a tunic and trousers obviously meant for someone else, being slightly longer than her in the leg and arms. It didn't matter, for she easily tied up the ends and fit her beautiful armor over all of it.

When she had only her helm left, she brushed her hair back with her hands and deftly tied it back with just a simple bit of cloth. Braids always came out anyway.

A knock sounded on the door, and she sheathed her sword quickly before saying, "Come."

Prince Adrian looked in, and then smiled widely.

She found herself grinning back at him, and then fiddled with the hilt of her sword. She didn't want him to know about the crack. She hoped that he thought it was healed as good as she had been. She didn't want anyone to know, but he had displayed such surety in her. She didn't want to disappoint him.

The door opened again, and Helena walked in, her eyebrows raising when she saw Clara, fully dressed for battle. "Clara, you shouldn't be out of bed!"

"I'm fine, Helena," she said. "Actually, better than fine, I spoke with the Lord, and He answered me. Adrian convinced me to try." She gestured at Adrian with a loose hand, as if trying to explain why he stood in her room with her.

"Good," Helena said, "but you are expected to stay here and heal fully."

"I am fully healed," Clara said, surprised Helena's reluctance.

"Clara, the poison from the serpent almost killed you," Helena said, almost scolding as she hung Clara's shield back on the weapons rack by the door.

"The Lord healed me, Helena, fully and completely," Clara said, and then she jumped lightly over the bed, and grabbed her shield. "I have to be in the battle today as Champion."

"The council and the battle commanders have already given their orders, and mine were to look out after you while you heal." Helena crossed her arms, and gave Clara her sternest look.

"Thank you, Helena," Clara said, putting her arm around her. "I appreciate your care and your concern. But the Lord healed me for a reason."

"I don't want to lose you too," said Helena softly, and she sniffled.

"I'm less lost now than I was a little while ago," said Clara.

"Please, Helena, I need to be in this battle, and I'll do my best to return."

Helena squeezed Clara tight, and ran out the door, wiping her cheeks with the back of her hand.

Clara sighed. "I don't want to hurt her, but my way is clear."

Adrian took her hand in his own, and simply said, "each of us has a destiny to fulfill, a purpose to which we have been given alone. I hope you know that no matter what happens . . ." his cheeks grew red.

Clara drew back a pace from him, disentangling her fingers. "No matter what happens later, we have a battle to get to right now." She marched past him trying to hide her own embarrassment, and out onto the deck. "We need to find out how quickly Captain Gurnsey can get us to Septily."

31 DECISIONS

Moments like these were such a sharp contrast to Stelia's time with the Drinaii that she couldn't help but think about them. In the Drinaii army, there were no councils. In the five years she had served as Captain, she had never once been allowed in any planning sessions. The Dark Sisterhood controlled the Drinaii, and Kalidess ruled over the Dark Sisterhood. All decisions were swift and final.

In contrast, the Allied Council spent hours discussing the inevitability of the upcoming battle. All options had been thoroughly thought over, even ones that involved running away and leaving the rest of the people of Septily to live under Kalidess's rule. Stelia had bitten her cheek until it bled during that discussion. She didn't think such an idea should be an option, not when she knew how Kalidess would use the population for her sacrifices and her sorcery. The Dark Sisterhood relied on magic drawn from blood and cruelty. The fear and misery of their victims seem to give them power. Even after her time with them, Stelia didn't understand fully why or how it could work, but it did somehow.

Finally, the council had reached the conclusion that battle was inevitable, and they could not allow Kalidess to stay in Septily. They had allowed the Dark Sisterhood to take over one tiny country after another in the southern lands and the eastern lands, and now they loomed threateningly over the last lands in the West. Septily, once seven kingdoms, was a large land, and from all the reports, Kalidess had concentrated her forces in the capital of Skycliff and the northern coastlands.

After what seemed an interminable time, the Allied forces had finally moved out, on ships and on griffin flyers to begin the battle to take back Septily. In the early hours of the morning, they had left Trader's Port, and sailed down the coastline. For the first few hours, Stelia stood next to Dantor in the bow of the ship they traveled aboard, taking comfort from his presence. Despite his injuries, he had regained his strength quickly, and had healed well under little Helena's healing blade. It seemed strange that such a thing as a blade could be part of any kind of healing, but Helena's green crystal blade held within it the power of the Lord than leant itself to healing.

However, the green crystal blade hadn't seemed to have much effect on Clara, and they had to leave her behind, unconscious still. Stelia worried inwardly over Clara's well-being. She let out a short sigh and tapped the table.

The Allied Council had decided to meet again, one more time, before the ships reached the coast, and the battle began. She couldn't imagine why all the councilors felt they had to have a say in military matters. Some of them were soft from pushing papers, and running the "affairs" of state, as they liked to say. Those sorts couldn't possible know what it meant to draw up battle plans and then find them blown to shreds once the enemy did something unexpected. The contingencies on a battlefield were too numerous to count, and one had to trust in the field commander to have a firm grasp of the situation and all the resources available to them.

Although Stelia wasn't found of joint field commanders, she felt thankful that the co-commanders would all fall under the decision of Master Theran, who had been among the refugees that had made their way to Port city with a small contingent of the Watch Guard. He had also escaped through the old city tunnels, but to the east of the city and not to the coast. He had brought with him reports of other refugees, and of the army of citizens that would help them take back the capital. Kalidess and her minions didn't seem to realize that

Septily had some independent thinkers among its working class people.

They had a fighting chance if they could sandwich Kalidess, the Dark Sisterhood and the Drinaii between the armies to the west of the city, and those that would be coming from the northern coastlands and the southern plains where another army was being put together by member by Triune Hall Sword Masters.

As she waited for yet another long council session to start, Stelia traced the seam of the folding table in front of her. The others were chatting in their little groups, comparing written notes and documents. She pulled out her favorite throwing knife and laid it on the table.

The room quieted, and she looked up. All eyes were riveted on the knife.

The short, stuffy ambassador from the Traders' Delegation said, "I hardly think that a knife is appropriate at a council table."

"Well, if it gets the lot of you to come to your points and give the final planning over to our field commander, then I find it highly appropriate," said Stelia firmly.

"Ahem," Shepherd Jordan cleared his throat. "Stelia does not of course speak for the whole Septilian delegation when she makes this statement." His normally gentle face was drawn in sharp lines of tension.

Stelia sighed. "I apologize, ladies and gentlemen, I know I am only a Sword-Scout for the Triune Halls, but we need to give the battle plans over to our field commander, and let him decide on tactics. A battle cannot be decided within a committee. Battles are fluid, and snap decisions will need to be made. One of my concerns is that Kalidess's forces are already on the move, and probably have been since before the attack on Skycliff."

A member of the Watch Guard stood, and leaned forward. "I agree with this Scout. We need to get this session under way, and we need to finalize the field commander's role. My reports that I will share in a moment only confirm what she has stated."

"How is it again that you know so much about Kalidess?" asked the same stuffy Trader delegate.

Stelia felt her gut tighten, but she kept her voice calm. "I was once her foster-daughter, her minion, and a Captain in the Drinaii forces. Every day was a torment, and I longed for escape. When my feelings became known and I tried to renounce the Dark Sisterhood, they tortured me and left me to die in the desert. Only through the aid of Shepherd Jordan and the Triune Halls of Septily did I survive." Stelia sighed. "I had hoped to be a valuable asset of information, but I can see that you do not trust me."

"Can you blame us?" asked a lean woman from the Trader delegation.

"Stelia's loyalty and faith are not an issue," said Shepherd Jordan.

"We of the Watch Guard agree," said the Watch-Guard representative.

"As do I," said Prince William, looking up from his notes.

"And as do we," said two voices from the wide doorway to the Captain's cabin. Two Aerlandian delegates in full uniform stood there, one human and one griffin. Too large to enter the cabin, the griffin had stayed outside with his head inside the door.

The other members of the council startled slightly. Some of them, Stelia realized, didn't seem to remember that the griffins were intelligent beings like themselves.

The griffin spoke again, "Although I am a student of prophecies, and I know that communication takes time between such different peoples, we must act now."

"The prophecies are clear," said the other Aerlandian delegate.

"The prophecies, the reports, and the advice we have from a trusted ally," said the Watch-Guard.

Stelia put the knife away in her belt in one smooth motion. "Thank you," she said. She turned to the Traders Delegation. "I apologize for my insensitivity, ladies and gentlemen."

The female delegate nodded slowly, recognizing her, but the stuffy man just shuffled his papers irritably.

"Call to Order," said the Watch-Guard.

"Agreed," intoned Stelia with the others. Finally, the meeting had at least started. The sooner started, the sooner finished, she hoped.

Master Theran stood by his seat, and raised his hands. "Trusted allies, we are thankful that you have come to the aid of our country in this time of darkness. Without you, we would be simple refugees, with no hope of recovering our capital, but with your aid we can overcome the darkness with the power of light that comes only from the Lord."

"Amen," said Shepherd Jordan, and Stelia found herself echoing him, along with most of the others in the room.

Master Theran nodded, and then looked somber. "As we have discussed and all of you know, our Champion has been struck down by poison, and is unable to stand by us during this time, but we have not given up hope, not in her, and not in the Lord. Prince Adrian, of the Aerlandian force, has stayed behind to stand watch over her, and to bring her to the battle if she recovers." He looked at the Aerlandian delegates by the door, and bowed slightly. "We thank you for his service."

"It is an honor to serve the Champion, and it is as the visions foretold Prince Adrian," said the human delegate, his face tight.

Stelia wondered why the man looked so worried, but she had a sinking feeling that she would find out.

Master Theran looked over the group. "We have asked, and I ask again, will you allow my leadership as field commander over the Allied Forces. The decision has been in your hands overnight, and I will gladly work with a sub-commander from each of your forces to ensure the safety of all our people."

The stuffy trader shuffled his papers, and then sat forward, and looked sideways at Prince William. "May I ask, does the Prince find this arrangement acceptable?"

Prince William's face colored slightly at the man's snide tone, but he nodded once and then stood to address the whole room. "Master Theran is the best qualified to be our field commander, having both experience and an intimate knowledge of the terrain of Septily." He looked at the trader carefully, and then around the room. "As you all know, my father has willingly placed himself under Kalidess' power. If we face him on the battlefield, I would wish Master Theran to make all decisions concerning him, for I do not wish to compromise our position with sentiment, or anger."

Stelia admired Prince William's candor and calm. He would make a wise ruler after his father, when the Triune Council approved of him, as she was sure that they would.

The female trader spoke now, with a glare at her colleague. "Thank you, Prince William, for your honesty. It sits with you well, and shows that you are a different man than your father. The Force from Trader's Port will submit to Master Theran's command."

"As will the Aerlandian Forces," said the griffin.

"And those from Destiny," said the Destinier delegate.

"And from the Watch Guard," said the Watch Guard by Stelia's right side.

"Thank you," said Master Theran. Then he took a deep breath, and said. "From this point on, I would like this meeting to be made up entirely of sub-commanders, and captains. We will lay out our battle plans, and discuss contingences."

"All in favor?" asked Shepherd Jordan.

"Aye," the majority said, although Stelia noted that the stuff trader delegate didn't look pleased. She stood up, ready to go, when Master Theran put his hand on her arm.

"I have a special task for you, Stelia," he said. "You should stay."

She nodded, and sat down again. She didn't relish the idea of another meeting, but at least war plans were more her specialty.

32 THE LAST SHIP

Adrian nearly bumped into Clara as she stopped short on the deck outside the healer's cabin.

"How long have we been in port?" she asked, clearly startled by the sight of the docks of Trader's Cove.

"Six nights, since the night after the attack," he told her. "We have Allied forces from Trader's Cove, Destiny Islands, Aerland, and the Watch Guard, as well as three forces of Septilian refugees. It seems your countrymen aren't going down without a fight."

"Good," she said, firmly, and then she slumped. "Only I hope . . . I hope not too many are getting hurt."

He put his hand on her shoulder again, wishing he could gather in his arms. How could he fall for the Champion, the one young woman that he couldn't have? All this time he had trained for battle, but he hadn't prepared himself for the intense feeling he felt from the first moment he had seen her. He had steeled himself for the fact that he most probably would die at the Champion's side, had used the inevitability of it as an excuse to justify all sorts of other wild stunts, and now he wanted to just live and hold her. But he couldn't tell her that, any of it.

"When your country needs you, when the Lord calls you, and when others are in danger, the act of sacrifice isn't something that you have to think about. It's just something you do. It's something that all of us find within us in the right time and place."

"Not everyone does," she said, "the Dark Sisterhood, the Drinaii, and all those who work for them don't sacrifice themselves." Clara said quietly.

"And that's what makes them servants of the darkness, and not of the Lord," he said.

"But they can change," said Clara, "I've seen it."

He squeezed her shoulder. "They can, but we can't wait for them to do that. We have to protect our people, the people of the Lord of light."

Clara nodded, and then reached up and squeezed his hand once before moving away from him.

Captain Gurnsey walked up to them.

"So it's to the battle, after all then," he said heartily. He nodded to Adrian and Kryssander. "With all the fancy flying and fighting going on, my crew and I have begun to feel left out." Then he took of his hat, and said quietly. "I never thought I would be giving my life into the Lord's hands after all that happened with Evalyn, but I see I've been in the wrong for a while now . . . heading towards the darkness just by being angry in my heart."

"The Lord's grace is enough," Clara said quietly. "Just trust Him."

"Aye," said Captain Gurnsey, "you're right." He nodded slowly. "I'll get the crew underway, and then I'll take a moment in my cabin to speak to Him about things, get my heart clean as Evalyn likes to say."

"Good," said Clara.

Captain Gurnsey began bellowing orders at his crew, and two slim figures raced down the rigging and across the deck to them.

"Clara, you're up and ready for battle!" shouted Rhodri as he ran up to her.

"Is it true? You aren't leaving us behind?" asked Helena right behind him. Her eyes were red from recent tears, but now they held a new sparkle.

Clara looked at Adrian, and shook her head slightly, but he shrugged in return, not knowing what to say. These younglings were of her people. Among the Aerlandians, children trained for battle from a much earlier age, but these two both had the look of scholars about them even if they did wear the golden armor of the Lord, and carry blades of power.

"I don't think that battle is the right place for you," Clara said slowly, "but I do think that you will be coming with us on the ship. I think," and she held up a hand to stall Helena, "that you would both serve best near the healing tents and not the battle lines."

Rhodri looked stubborn, but Helena frowned thoughtfully.

"I had planned to fly with Clara when we get closer to the shoreline, until we reach the very front lines," said Adrian. "I'm sure that they'll need her where the fighting is at its worst, and Kryss can only take two riders." He waved to Kryssander, who sauntered over to their group.

"The angel who saved me," whispered Clara, obviously awed.

"He's no angel, but he will fly us to the battle," said Adrian, giving his friend a wink.

"No angel?" Kryss shouldered Adrian playfully. "I suppose not." Then he turned to Clara. "I am Kryssander, of the 12th Wing," said Kryss, bowing to her. "I am pleased to meet you again and under better circumstances, Champion Clara."

"Thank you, Kryssander, for saving my life," she said. "I am pleased to meet you as well." She bowed slightly in return. When she raised her head, she had tears in her eyes. "I always dreamed I would fly, and now . . . well, I didn't expect it would be like this."

"Life is never exactly what we expect it to be, even with prophecies guiding our steps," said Kryssander. He glanced at Adrian.

Adrian nodded, trying to reassure his friend that Clara had faith, and that they would be all right. "Clara is ready for the battle."

"And we are too," said Rhodri. Helena nodded firmly, and looked at Clara.

"If anything happened to either of you, I wouldn't know what to do, and I would feel responsible," said Clara softly. "I can't risk it."

"You will have to," Kyrssander said firmly. "This morning, I had a vision. It was hazy about many things, but I know that these young ones will be needed near the battle on one of the ships. So sure is my vision that I have found a friend to help them," he said, and then he nodded towards the sky.

A young griffin soared towards them, slowing for a landing. Smaller in neck and body, with dark gray markings and wide green eyes, Hashani was the youngest flyer attached to the 12th Wing, usually a messenger and not a fighter.

"Hashani, it's good to see you again, little flyer," said Adrian in welcome.

"I am glad to be of help, especially in my training year," Hashani said in a lilting high voice. She tilted her head curiously at Clara, Helena and Rhodri. "It is nice to meet you Champion . . . and these must be the young ones I have heard about. I understand you will fly to battle with me, when the ship is closer to shore."

"Yes," shouted Rhodri.

"Yes, Hashani," said Helena shyly. She bowed politely to Hashani and then approached her slowly. "May I touch your feathers?"

"You may," she said, raising her ear tufts and tilted her head the other way. The three of them wandered over to the side of the ship, speaking in quiet tones.

Adrian watched as Hashani made sure her two younger charges were comfortable with her, and he put a hand on Kryss' neck, "Remember when . . ."

"Yes," said Kryss. "You were a bit more like the boy than the girl, pushing your way to the front of the fledging ground."

"I had hoped you would pick me," said Adrian.

"I know," said Kryss, and then he looked over at Clara. "In Aerland, the flyers choose their human partners, sometimes at the fledging and sometimes after training. Hashani has yet to choose her partner, and we thought she may be a messenger for all time. However, it might make for a stronger alliance, to have young ones become flyer partners."

"It might," said Clara, obviously surprised. "I admit I hadn't thought that far ahead." She blushed slightly. "I usually do what is before me, and leave the planning to others. I'm afraid that I've been terrible at tactics classes." Then she touched the pommel of her sword. "Yet somehow, I'm the Champion . . . I'm not really sure why."

"Each Champion is unique, talented in his or her own way, to give glory to the Lord," said Kryss.

"You're the right Champion for this time and this place," said Adrian. He wanted to add, for me, but he knew that he couldn't so he settled for just gazing at her blue eyes and her flyaway tresses and wished that he could have just one more day more than this.

Clara blushed slightly, and looked away from him. Adrian took a step towards her, but Kryss nudged grabbed the back of his shirt with his beak. "We need to talk," Kryss said quietly.

Clara glanced over at them, and then said, "I'll let you two have some time. I need to pray some more before the battle." She looked somber and sad, but determined.

Adrian wanted to follow her as she walked across the deck to take a seat up in the bow of the ship, but Kryss still held his shirt. "What is it, Kryss?"

Kryss gave him a small shake and then let go of him. "You're my best friend, and this is our last day, or could be our last day together. I know she's beautiful by human standards, but that girl is tied up with our fate. She needs to pray and concentrate before battle, and not have a love-sick prince following her around."

"I'm not a love-sick prince," Adrian said. "I just . . . well, I didn't expect to feel the way that I do around her." He felt his face grow hot, and turned to face Kryss, gazing into his friend's bright green eyes. "I think she's going to be all right," he said.

"She just spent seven days sleeping, and her sword lost its power in the midst of that last battle. She looks shaky to me," said Kryss.

"What are you saying? That we shouldn't go with her to battle?" asked Adrian, crossing his arms. "After all that training, all these years, you want to fly away and ignore the call that we've been given?"

Kryss clacked his beak in irritation, and clawed at the deck, leaving gouges. "No, I do not!"

Sailors around them stopped their work, and Adrian could understand why. An angry griffin wasn't something most people wanted to face. However, despite the gouges the deck, Adrian knew that Kryss could keep himself under control. "Then what are you saying?" he asked.

Kryss closed his eyes. "I want to spend the day with you, my friend. I want to fly and feel the wind under my wings without a battle raging around us, just one last time."

Adrian put his hand out, and touched the soft feathers under Kryss's ear. "Then let's fly, my friend."

Kryss made half-purr, half-chirruping sound of happiness, and then opened his eyes. "Thank you."

When Kryss knelt down, Adrian slid into the light saddle and strapped his legs into the straps. He had a feeling that Kryss wanted to do some acrobatics.

With three short steps and a heavy beat of his wings, Kryss launched into the air, clearing the railing and soaring up into the sky. The dark clouds were heavy above them, and damp air clung to them, but Kryss's flight took them up and through the clouds into the bright sky above.

33 FLIGHT

In the bow of the ship, Clara tried to clear her mind of any distractions. Adrian and Kryssander were both distracting in their own way. The griffin's beauty and strength left her in awe, and the boy, the prince, well, he left her feeling full of butterflies and awkwardness. She didn't have time for such things, and she didn't know him well enough. Her parents were gone, she was on the way to the nightmarish battle of her visions, and her sword was cracked. Kryss looked too much like the griffin in her nightmares, the one that died. She hoped that she was wrong. She hoped that somehow she could change what happened in the nightmares and win the battle. So she prayed, and cleared her mind, and prayed again.

Time passed, and she could feel her muscles begin to cramp from sitting in one position for too long. She sighed slightly and stretched. She had to warm up her muscles as well as her mind, but as she stood she realized she was hungry. It seemed like such an odd thing, such a normal thing, with a battle on the horizon of her thoughts.

As she turned to leave the fore castle, she saw Evalyn coming up the short ladder with a small tray.

"I thought you might like something to eat," the former mermaid said, setting the tray down on the deck, and then sitting by it. There were two sandwiches, and two small cups of water.

"Thank you," Clara said. She sat down on the other side of the tray, and then bowed her head to pray.

When she finished praying, she looked up to see Evalyn holding a dark comb in her hands.

"Is that the one that ensorcelled you?" Clara asked.

"Yes," Evalyn said, sighing. "I can't seem to figure out how to dispose of it. We tried to burn it the other day, and James thinks we should throw it into the sea."

"James?"

Evalyn smiled. "Captain Gurnsey's first name is James."

"Oh," Clara said, feeling a little foolish. "Why haven't you tossed it overboard then?"

"I'm afraid it would be a snare to some other unsuspecting person if it ever came to shore," Evalyn said. Then she looked out over the railing towards the sea. "The ocean has a way of bringing things back to us when we least expect it, both the good and the bad."

"I hadn't thought of that," said Clara. She gazed at the comb, and then put her hand out. "May I?"

Evalyn held the comb close to her and then reluctantly offered it. "Be careful," she said. "It isn't just another object, there's a feeling when you hold it, a feeling of . . . I don't know how to describe it."

Clara took the comb in her hands, and almost dropped it. The thing burned, and yet pulled at her. She swallowed, and then put it down purposefully on the deck and drew her sword. When she touched the blade to the comb, a bright flash burned the comb to a pile of ashes.

Evalyn let out a ragged sigh. "Thank you." She sighed again. "It felt like it was calling to me, like I had to put it on again, and now . . . that feeling is gone. Thank you." Then she bent and looked closely at the sword. "Is that a crack?"

Clara closed her eyes, and then opened them again. "It is." She swallowed, and then picked up one of the cups of water and eased the pain in her throat. "I think, that somehow it's a consequence of my doubt, or a test of my faith. I'm not sure which."

"What will it mean for the coming battle?" asked Evalyn.

Clara sheathed the sword, and this time it was her turn to sigh. "I don't know. I've had nightmares and visions, and I just don't know why I have been called to live out the prophecy that you spoke."

"When darkness fills seas and lands,
A young girl born in the sands
Will bring the light of the sword
To the people of the Word.
If poisoned by doubt the sword will break,
The storm will rise, the lightning speak.
When faith is pure, the sword will remain
The Champion will save the Lord's domain.
A defender and a healer she will be
If she accepts her destiny."

Clara listened to the words again, and she shook her head. "It doesn't help knowing these things."

"I'm sorry, Clara, I should never have told you," Evalyn said.

"No, there's a reason that I know it now, and a reason for these visions. I just don't understand it yet," Clara said. Then she looked down at the sandwiches. "I do know that I'm hungry though, and I need to be prepared for battle physically, as well as mentally." She took a bite of one of the sandwiches, and focused on the savory flavor of meat and spices. "Thank you, Evalyn."

Hours later, after stretching and warming up, Clara watched Kryssander and Adrian land carefully on the deck. They had flown away from the ship in the morning, and we're just now arriving back. She hoped they were going to be rested enough for the battle.

When she voiced her concerns, Adrian just smiled. "Oh, Kryss just wanted to spend a little time with me. We actually stopped on a tiny island, more of a rock than an island, had our lunch and watched some birds for a while."

Clara couldn't imagine why a majestic griffin would want to spend the day before a battle watching birds, but she could see that they both looked fresh and ready.

Kryssander cocked his head towards the distant shoreline. "We near the Septilian section of the coast, and I see our ships at anchor."

Clara followed his gaze, and could just make out the land mass, but not the ships. She realized that a griffin's eyes must be especially keen, like a hawk's eyes. Although she didn't think she could ever be prepared for what lay ahead, she had all that she needed: her armor, her sword, and her faith, small as it seemed at the moment.

Adrian, on the other hand, still wore a tunic, shirt, and trews, with only a short sword at his side. "I'll get my gear," he said hastily, and ran down the stairs that led below decks.

Kryssander paced slowly closer to Clara, and then cocked his head slightly at her. "You have been much in his thoughts, and mine. This battle is a culmination of many years of training in response to the Lord's visions and prophecies for both of us. He bowed his head low. "It will be an honor to fulfill those visions."

"Thank you," Clara said. She bowed her head to him, as well, not sure how else to respond to his words. She wondered if his visions had been nightmares like hers, but from the intense gleam in his eyes, she wasn't sure she dared to ask.

When everyone had gathered together, Clara watched as Adrian helped Rhodri and Helena into small riding saddles fitted around Hashani's middle. They both clutched at the saddle pommels as Adrian put a strap around their legs.

"This strap is here to keep you in the saddle in case Heshani has to make sudden moves in the battle," Adrian explained to them.

"But won't we be on the ground for the battle?" asked Helena.

"You might be, or you might stay aloft, depending on the situation," said Adrian. "I'm sure that the Lord will guide us and keep you safe." He looked over at Kryssander, "Isn't that right, Kryss?"

"Their role will be important, but I didn't get all the details in my vision."

"Visions are like that," said Rhodri, as if he knew all about them.

Considering all that had happened to them, and how little Clara had spoken to him, she supposed he might know more than her. He had been a Shepherd student before all this had happened.

Behind him, Helena fingered the leg straps and then looked at

Clara, "May the Lord lift you up on wings like eagles, Champion." She smiled brightly and then leaned. "I'm ready, Hashani."

"Me too," said Rhodri.

Hashani cocked her head in a griffin smile, and then she began to beat her wings in the air. After a few minutes of warming up, she took several running steps forward and launched into the air over the rail of the cog.

Clara watched them for a moment, feeling amazed at the bravery of the two young students. Of course, anyone watching a griffin take flight would want to fly. It seemed like the most natural longing in the world.

"Ready for wings, Clara?" asked Adrian from behind her.

She turned, and saw that Adrian had already mounted Kryssander.

Captain Gurnsey and Evalyn walked swiftly across the deck towards them.

"Thank you," said Evalyn, and then she embraced Clara in a tight hug. "Thank you for saving me, Clara. Stay safe."

"I'll try," said Clara, hugging her back.

Captain Gurnsey shook her hand heartily with a broad smile, and then it was time to go. Clara turned to Kryssander, not really sure how to go about getting into the saddle.

Kryssander crouched, and Adrian held out his hand. She clasped his forearm, put her foot in the rear stirrup, and swung into the temporary saddle behind him. Adrian showed her how to strap on the leg straps, and she looked for a pommel to hold onto. There was nothing in front of her except Adrian. She felt too close suddenly.

Kryssander took three giant steps and then a leap into the air, fanning out his enormous wings and beating them against the air. With lurching jolts, they climbed slowly and laboriously upwards. Clara could hear Kryssander's breathing and feel it between her legs. "Is this going to be all right, for him to carry two?" she asked Adrian, leaning in and holding onto him so he could hear her over the wing beats.

"I'll be fine," Kryssander answered, gulping air. "It's taking off with two from a short start that's difficult." He seemed to have reached a decent height, well above the crow's nest, and he dove slightly and the swooped upward, riding the wind. Clara clung to Adrian during this maneuver, burying her cheek into his shoulder and squeezing her legs for more balance.

"Much as I am enjoying you close to me," Adrian said, "you really don't have to hold on like that."

"Oh," Clara said, glad that he couldn't see her ears burning red in embarrassment. She relaxed her grip on him and Kryssander little by little, until she felt comfortable. Gazing out over the water, she could just see the edge of the mainland. She wasn't sure if she should look down. She loved the feel of the cold air biting her cheeks and running through her hair, the wonder of being so high in the sky. "It's so glorious!" she said.

"Yes, it is," Adrian said.

She felt his hand cover her left one, where she gripped his waist. He curled his fingers around hers, and held her hand. She felt an urge to pull away from him. She still really didn't know him that well. But at this moment, on the eve of battle, with her nightmares in the back of her mind, and the tiny crack in her sword weighing on her heart, she decided to lean into him and lay her head against his shoulder.

When they neared the mainland, Clara could make out several ships, and many people on the shore. Beyond them, not far enough away, an army was encamped on the hillside leading up to the mainland of Septily. It wasn't as steep as it was closest to Skycliff, but the enemy had the high ground, and it looked like the battle had already started.

They were nearly caught up to Hashani, Rhodri, and Helena, who appeared to be talking to one another. They were pointing at the battle.

Clara straightened in her seat. "Where should we engage the enemy?"

"Clara," Adrian said quietly. "There's something you should know about the visions that Kryss and I have had."

His voice gentle, but Clara dreaded hearing his next words. She didn't want to know if his vision and her nightmare coincided. She didn't want it to happen. She wouldn't let it happen. "I don't want visions and prophecies to cloud my judgment," she said sternly.

He drew in his breath quickly, and went silent. Finally, he exhaled slowly. "I understand your choice, Champion." He leaned forward and away from her. "Where shall we go, Kryss?"

"Hashani should go to the ships, and we will go to the right flank, up the hill a ways. Do you see that fiery light about midway up, with the mass of soldiers around it?"

"Yes, I can just make out a fire . . . is it a bonfire?"

"No," said Kryssander. "I'm not sure what it is, but it has the shape of a man on fire."

Fear and dread clenched in Clara's stomach. "No," she whispered.

"You see him, Champion?" asked Kryss.

Clara shook her head and swallowed.

"Clara?" asked Adrian.

"Send the young ones to the ships. Drop me where I can reach the burning man. Stay safe. Harry them from above. Let me fight him on my own." It all came out stilted and in a rush, but Kryssander seemed to understand her.

They had reached the younger group now, and he gave orders to Hashani. Clara could hear Helena and Rhodri wishing them well, and she raised her hand and nodded, unable to speak. Her nightmare might be about to come true.

34 THE POWER OF PAIN

Roaring filled his ears. Pain covered his body. Agony wrapped around his soul. Alexandros struck out against the roaring, the pain, the agony, and he felt his sword arm come into contact with something. He heard screams: the screams of his enemies. But it didn't give him joy. He felt only sorrow, only pain, only agony and confusion. He struck blindly against it all again and again, but it never ceased.

In her lacquered chariot on the highest point of the hill, Kalidess watched the battle unfold with satisfaction. Finally, the fool of a king would meet his end, all the while striking down his own people and her enemies. She licked her lips at the smell of blood, and the screams of pain. It was all coming together perfectly. Her sisters were lined up along the hill just below her, with their bare feet against the ground, soaking up the power that could come only through suffering.

Her own power, rooted through all those she had contracted with, poured into her from their pain, whether it was physical or emotional. Either way, she gained while they lost. The power coming from Alexandros' anguish could last her years.

For now, the battle was in her favor, from the high ground, through the Drinaii forces, and the magic of her dark sisters, who were at this point bringing in a storm of weather over the battlefield.

The skies were growing black, as the clouds covered the sun. A heavy, suffocating warmth was in the air, and then the thunder roiled.

Lightning cracked down, and one of her dark sisters sent it against one of the ships. It hit the mast, and the ship buckled beneath the power.

The creatures of Aerland were landing. They couldn't last long in air with the rain pouring down on them. But one griffin kept coming on towards the hill, to the right of Alexandros' position. She wondered what the feathered twit thought it could gain there.

35 AT THE EDGE

When Master Theran, riding in on the Destinier Ship named Hope, had seen the forces of the Dark Sisterhood and the Drinaii arrayed on high ground above their planned landing place, he had signaled for a stop. The ships had slowed and turned, staying back from the shore. A hasty planning committee went to work with Master Theran, and then the ships put to shore slightly further up the coast.

When Stelia gazed at the enemy lines, she felt overwhelmed, and then angry. When she had heard her orders, she ground her teeth, and made sure that everyone in her unit was prepared. Salene and Dantor would flank Prince William at all times. Although Prince William and Dantor both outranked her, Master Theran placed her as sergeant of their unit, expecting her to keep Prince William safe. Dantor accepted her lead for their unit easily, and so did the others, even those few Sword Guards she didn't know personally. Privately, she wondered if Master Theran's decision came about partially to both show his trust in her, and to keep her away from Kalidess.

She didn't want to be captured again, and wouldn't allow herself to be captured alive, but she wished she had a reason to charge the battle line with those in the front. She would like to take a chunk out of the enemy forces. None of their captive's tales of the Dark Sisterhood's growing power had prepared them for what lay ahead of them.

Six centuries of Drinaii troops lined the hillside, with six Dark Sisters overseeing them. Kalidess stood in a chariot on the top of the hill, holding a dark staff in one hand, and the reins of her horses in the other. She was too far away for Stelia to see her, but Stelia knew the way Kalidess liked to oversee her battles from a high point, directing her troops through the Dark Sisterhood and the Drinaii Captains.

The Allied Forces numbered only four hundred, combining Destiniers, Traders, Septilian refugees, and Watch Guards into four groups, with three Aerlandian Wings planning to take to the air. They were outnumbered two to one.

Stelia's unit was near the rear of their allied army, closest to the ships. From where they landed, they would need to march towards the enemy, and Stelia could understand Master Theran's decision to take them to the northern side, hoping to gain distance and engage from the side. Stelia wondered if it would have been better to wait for another day, or to try a different section of the coast, but she wasn't in command and she accepted her role. Before they had deployed from the ships, there had been a time of prayer, and just one shout. "For the Lord, For the Light!"

Ashore, the front lines had started at a steady march, but the first unit shouted their battle cry once more, and then broke into a run. Stelia glanced at Master Theran, and saw his face grimace. That hadn't been part of the plan then.

The front unit started with heavy momentum but became overwhelmed by the Drinaii within a few minutes of fighting. The Aerlandians were a great source of help, diving down and shooting arrows into the Drinaii forces. The second unit joined the first, and the fighting stalled on the hillside, with neither force gaining any ground.

Stelia glanced at her mini-unit of seven, and noticed that they were all wrapped up in the intensity of the battle, fingers on their weapons, itching to join in the fight. But she had her orders, and hoped that they remembered them too. They were to keep Prince William at the rear lines, only to engage if their forces tipped the scales and began to take the battle.

"Please," Prince William pleaded with her, his eyes huge with concern. He wanted to fight, he didn't have to say anything else.

She knew how he felt. "We advance behind the rear unit," she said, giving in slightly. They began to march forward, and she felt her cheeks burning. Commander Theran was probably displeased. She kept their pace slow, and continued to watch the battle. It seemed like it was becoming dimmer, and she glanced up at the sky.

Dark clouds were forming overhead, bunching together to block out the sun.

Kalidess had put everything into this battle, as if she knew they were coming, and they were giving her exactly what she wanted: more victims for her sorcery that fed off of pain and death. Stelia stopped Prince William and their mini-unit with a held up hand, and she looked back at Master Theran. Did he know? Did he truly understand how Kalidess' power worked?

Stelia also wondered why Kalidess had such a desire to conquer Septily. As she waited, with the others, as the battle inched closer to them, she thought about the history of Septily that she knew. When Septily had formed, when Champion Elar had forced back the powers of darkness and that darkness had been led by a force of evil sorceresses . . . the beginnings of the Dark Sisterhood perhaps.

Stelia shook her head. Now was not the time to understand why, now it was the time to survive.

Suddenly the air grew heavy, and hot. Darkness crept over them. The black thunderclouds filled the sky.

She realized that even with their small bit of progress, they were still standing on wet sand, and this suddenly seemed very wrong.

"Get into the dry sand," she shouted to the others. She yanked on Prince William's arm, and dragged him forward and to the left of the battle into the dry sand.

Thunder boomed, and a dark bolt of sorcerous lightning struck the nearest galleon. The ship rocked. Another blast hit the water, and the surface of the water and the wet sand crackled.

A few stragglers from one of the other units screamed and fell to the ground. They had been standing in the wet sand, and the lightning overwhelmed them.

Master Theran had run forward with her group with a few of his men beside him, and panted to a stop near her. "Dear Lord," he breathed.

"What of the Rusty Way? Is she safe, do you think?" asked Salene.

Stelia looked across the water at the Rusty Way Galleon, where the healers and the students were waiting to take on wounded soldiers. The ship, deemed a place of safety, looked vulnerable now. "I hope so," she said. "As long as they don't take a direct hit, they should be safe."

As she watched the ship, a small griffin flew up to it and landed on its vast deck. Two small figures got off the griffin's back, and they all raced to shelter under the foc'sle. Could that have been Clara? But no, the smallest figure had dark hair . . . Helena?

Stelia turned her head, scanning the sky just in time to catch the flight of another griffin streaking towards the battlefield. While most of the griffins and their riders were landing to get out of the storm, this one flew towards the right flank, about midway up the hillside. She could just make out the glow of a sword on the back rider. "Clara, no," she whispered. The girl couldn't possibly be well enough to engage in battle.

Stelia looked to her unit and Commander Theran, stricken with the need to get to Clara's side and help her, or stop her.

"I saw her too," said Salene, her face set and worried. "But I need to stay with Prince William."

"Leave the Prince and our group to me," said Dantor, grimly. "I would go if I could, but my leg isn't healed enough for that climb." He shook his head. "I was a fool to come."

"No," she said, going to him. She ran his hand over the section of his cheek under his helmet visor. "You have never been a fool, Dantor." She nodded to him. "You are the right man at the right time, as always, Dantor."

She swallowed and glanced at Master Theran. He nodded once, and said, "Go, she'll need you."

"Thanks, I'd like to take someone to guard my back," she looked at the others.

A young sword guard from the Forester province nodded to her. "I'll go," he said.

"Good," she said, relieved to have one fellow sword master to watch her back.

With one last look at Dantor, she turned and started to run towards the right flank, skirting the furthest edges of the battle. She continued to scan the battle as she climbed the hill at a jog, hearing the young sword master panting behind her. In any other circumstance she might slow down for him, but she couldn't. Any time wasted could mean Clara's life.

36 NIGHTMARE BATTLE

The scene below came out of the background of Clara's worst nightmares. Septily's forces and their allies battled the Drinaii all over the sandy hillside covered in small, hardy bushes and rocky outcrops.

Kyrssander dove down behind the jumble of rocks nearest the burning man who struck at his foes in a roaring rage.

Clara hugged Adrian, and then jumped down. "Thank you," she said. Then she turned to Kryssander, "Thank you both." She paused for a moment, looking at both of them.

Adrian's wind-tousled hair seemed out of place over his set expression. He leaned down and touched her cheek. "Remember me, Clara."

"Remember us," said Kryssander, brushing against her arm with his wing.

She swallowed on a dry throat, trying to hold back tears. "I will." Then she bowed to them both.

When she looked up, Kryssander was bunching his muscles and beating his wings.

She stepped back, and he took several paces and took off, into the winds of the storm.

"O Lord, please," she whispered. She hoped things would be different than her vision but she didn't know if they could be. Was it up to her? She didn't know, and she couldn't wait for an answer.

Drawing two throwing knives, she started stalking towards the edge of the battle. Crouched low behind scrubby bushes, she managed to get close the edge of the fighting without being noticed. She threw her knives quickly, going through her whole bandolier in a few minutes. Most of her knives found marks in the enemy, either wounding them, or sending them down with a fatal strike. She didn't take too much time to watch the aftermath.

She swung her shield to the front, and gripped the handles firmly. With her right hand she drew the sword of power. It dimly lit the darkness that threatened the hillside. She took a deep breath, and started to run towards the burning man, hacking and slashing her way against the enemy as she went. She didn't stop to engage anyone, but continued forward, determined in her course.

A mace flew down towards her, and she blocked it with her shield and rolled free. In one smooth motion, she returned to her feet, and started moving forward again. The fighting grew thicker, and her pace slowed as she fought with one enemy after another. The sword's light remained low, but she could feel the power thrumming through her, and every move in each fight seemed choreographed like a dance. The Drinaii fell before her, and she didn't know how many she killed or wounded. She didn't feel anger, or fear, but a strange sort of peace, with that continued need to push forward to her goal.

Finally, the burning man was only a few paces away, and she could see the Allies of Septily falling back before his fiery sword strokes and his frightening visage.

The burning man's sword flamed to a length of six feet, but the man wielded it as if it were a normal sword. His whole upper body was encased in flame, and Clara could see fire licking at his legs. An inarticulate roaring came from his mouth, which looked surprisingly whole inside the flames. His eyes were burned shut, and his hair was blackened, but on his head he wore a crown. Clara paused for a moment as she realized that the burning man was King Alexandros. The spell that consumed him seemed to have driven him completely mad. His fighting wasn't controlled or skilled, just random and sweeping. However, everything in his path burned.

She hesitated for a moment more, and another Drinaii soldier swung at her with a curved sword. She parried, and thrust back at him, dealing with the immediate threat but also thinking of the King. Could she free him from the sword? Would that change the destiny of her dreams? She didn't know.

Her lack of attention almost got her killed as the Drinaii swordsman came inside her guard with an unexpectedly long lunge.

She jumped back, jostling someone behind her. She ducked, and crabbed sideways as the Drinaii swung at her and hit the Watch Guard woman she had jostled. The woman cried out in pain, but she pressed forward, thrusting her sword into his enemy even as she fell.

Clara couldn't wait any longer. She knew that the King was the key to this battle. With a new determination, she charged him, swinging not at his body, but at his sword arm, determined to part it from his body.

He parried with a wide sweep that sent small sparks of fire along her blade.

Clara's blade grew brighter, and Clara riposted, pushing against the fiery blade with a move that normally would knock a blade from a man's fingers.

He circled his wrist, and thrust forward.

She parried with her shield and sidestepped, cutting down at his arm.

Her blade sunk into his arm, but the King merely shrugged her off and back up a step. The flames on his arm leapt higher, and when they died down, his arm was whole.

Clara felt the beginning of fear start to creep up on her. The blade dimmed slightly, and the darkness around them grew in strength. Women's voices chanted in a twisted language from the hilltop. Dark lightning struck the earth on Clara's left side, and she jumped out of its way and towards the King's sword which was sweeping towards her. She brought her own sword up just in time, and then heard a crackling noise.

The King hammered another blow down at her, and she raised

her shield. Her legs buckled under the strength of his blow.

His sword came down again and again, striking against her shield. Her left arm went numb from the pain, and she felt pushed down into the wet muddy sand. She couldn't take the blows much longer, so she raised her sword again, and tried to parry his down stroke. The sword snapped, and the crystal blade flew away. Clara screamed as the fiery sword came down on her arm. She rolled and brought the shield up, cowering beneath it, clutching the hilt of her broken sword against her waist. She couldn't move her blackened fingers, and they remained clenched around the pommel.

Despair overwhelmed her and she wept as the ensorcelled king rained down one strike after another on her shield. She knew that at some point, she would no longer be able to hold the shield above her head. The pain on her wrist radiated up her arm, and the muddy sand covered her leggings. The dark storm rolled and struck around her.

A piercing shriek of anger rose above the sounds of the storm, and the King stopped his attack. She looked over the edge of her shield to see Kryssander diving down towards them, with Adrian on his back, throwing knife after knife at the King. Terror seized her. Her nightmare was coming true.

Kryssander's white and gold feathers streaked boldly against the stormy skies as he dove down at King Alexandros, his claws outstretched to strike.

The King, burning and seemingly blind, swung his sword instinctively above him, as if he sensed the attack. His blade burned through one of Kryssander's claws, but Kryssander's momentum sent him crashing into the King and they both went down into the sandy mud of the hillside, rolling towards Clara.

Adrian leaped clear of his saddle and grabbed Clara by her wrist, dragging her to one side just in time to avoid being crushed by the combined weight of the griffin and the King, locked in battle.

Clara felt numb with fear as the events of her nightmares unfolded in front of her. Dark lightning struck the ground next to Adrian, and she pulled him towards her.

He touched her face with his hand, and smiled lopsidedly for a moment. "I always wondered what I would feel when I met you, Champion," he said, leaning close to her ear. "Now I know." He kissed her lightly on the cheek, and then stepped away from her, towards the King.

She wanted to say something to him, to stop him, but she couldn't.

The piercing cry of a dying hawk rose above the clash of battle, and Clara watched in horror as King Alexandros cut his way through Kryssander's body and started to come down the hillside again. His roaring hadn't ceased, and he still swung his sword wildly.

Adrian intercepted him, with his short sword, leaping in and out of the King's range, trying to confuse him. The fight between them went on longer than Clara expected, with the King's swings following no set pattern. Unfortunately, Adrian was unable to hurt him and Adrian was wearing down.

Clara looked down at the broken sword in her hands. A jagged edge of crystal stood above the hilt, and it was dim, like a plain river stone. She sucked in a breath, and then let it out. Somehow she had to have faith. She had to fight. She had to find a way to turn this battle for her people, and for the Lord. She slowly walked towards the fight between the King and Adrian, and started to pace around them looking for a way to help Adrian.

A Drinaii swung his sword at her, and she knocked it away with her shield, and then rammed him with the flat of her shield hitting him in the temple.

Looking back at the fight between the King and Adrian, she saw an opening and took it.

Lunging towards the King's back with her shield, she caused him to stumble but his wild backhand swing almost hit her in the head.

Adrian struck the King in the front, but the flames reached towards him as they healed the King, and Adrian cried out, dropping his short sword.

The King raised his sword and struck at Adrian, and Adrian

retreated with his shield above his head.

"No," Clara yelled, and she hit the King again with her shield, barely avoided the flames that encased him.

He ignored her and continued to advance on Adrian.

She went around him, and tried to get between them.

The King's sword came down at her, and she raised her shield. Before the blow could strike her, Adrian threw himself between them, holding his short sword in his left hand. He stabbed into the King, and the King sliced down at him as he staggered back.

"Trust in the light, Clara," Adrian called out to her. "Trust in the Lord's light." His clothes were on fire, and he dropped to the ground.

The King advanced, and the chanting of the women grew above the sounds of the battle and the storm.

"Trust the light," Clara said. She looked at the jagged hilt of her sword, and saw a tiny glow. She didn't have anything left. Dropping her battered shield, she put both hands around the hilt of her sword, and thrust it towards the sky. "Lord, you are my light," she shouted. "You are my strength, and my shield, my sword, and my deliverer."

The light from the shattered sword exploded into brilliance, throwing everything else into shadow. Clara felt filled with a power that thrummed through her and filled her with peace.

Jagged dark lightning came down towards her, but she stood firm, and the light from the sword reached up and broke through the clouds, scattering them apart.

The chanting stopped, as the light broke into streams and struck the Dark Sisters on the hillside. Then the light went out in a wave over the battlefield, rolling over everyone around Clara and out to the edges. It sounded like a wave crashing onto the beach, and left only silence in its wake.

When the light receded, Clara stood with her face up to the sky. "Thank you, Lord," she said. "Thank you."

Looking around her she saw her countrymen and their allies on their feet, while the Drinaii and the Dark Sisters had all fallen. In front of her, the King lay in the mud, no longer on fire, but obviously burned from the waist up. He whimpered and moaned.

Just behind him, Adrian lay on the ground, his face pale.

Clara went to him, her heart beating hard in her chest. She knelt down and put her hand on his face, pushing his helm back.

He opened his eyes, and smiled a small smile. "You were worth it, Clara. You were worth it all. You are the Champion. You . . ." he stopped speaking and closed his eyes in pain, clutching at his side.

"Adrian." Clara tried to pull his hand away to look at his wound, but he resisted her.

He gasped, and his eyes looked beyond her. "The light is so beautiful."

Clara turned to look over her shoulder, but she didn't see anything other than a blue sky overhead. When she turned back to him, his eyes were glazed and fixed on some spot she couldn't see, and she realized he had stopped breathing.

"No," she cried, the tears flowing down her cheeks. "No, not you too," she whispered into his shoulder as she leaned over him, holding him even as his body grew cold. She knew he was gone, the part of him that mattered had already moved on, but she stayed there crying, until Stelia found her.

37 AFTERMATH

When the light banished the darkness, Stelia had been almost there, almost to the battle between the burning man and Clara. She had seen Kryssander and Adrian's sacrifice. She had seen Clara stand and lift the broken blade above her head. She was running towards them at full speed, when the light struck her and everyone around her. She was blinded by it, and yet her eyes stayed open, drinking it in somehow. She went still, and felt the warmth of the light press into her, and around her, and then it receded.

As she stood still, trying to take stock of her bearings, she noticed Clara run to Adrian's side. Stelia hesitated a moment more, and looked around the battlefield. The Drinaii were down, but slowly getting up, crawling away from the Septilians in fear. Piles of ash and swirls of smoke marked where the Dark Sisters had stood on the hill, with one exception.

Kalidess's black lacquered chariot had turned and was speeding away from the scene of the battle, with Kalidess flicking her whip on her horses' backs, urging them away.

Stelia wanted to chase her down and finish her off, but then she looked at Clara again, and she knew that Kalidess would have to come later. She cleaned off her sword, and sheathed it, walking towards Clara slowly.

As she passed the burnt man, she realized with horror that it was King Alexandros, now moaning and whimpering in pain, curled on the ground in a fetal position. She couldn't leave him there, so she turned to find the sword guard who had followed her. He stood, obviously in shock, back where she had stopped running when the light hit them.

She went to him, and tapped him on the shoulder.

He was gulping for air, his eyes wide, but he shook himself and nodded to her.

"Get a healer up here," she said.

"Yes, sir," he said, and then he sheathed his sword, and started running back the way they had come, obviously glad for something specific to do.

Stelia wasn't surprised. A lot of people reacted that way to something out of the ordinary. They didn't know how to handle their own reaction, but given something to do, they would gladly take on some normal task and do it well as a way of coping.

She went back to Clara, and knelt down next to her. This wasn't her area of expertise. Not really. She could encourage apprentices to fight, but comfort them when they were sick or heartbroken? She didn't think she had the words. So she simply reached out and put her hand on Clara's back.

Clara jumped a little, and then took a shaky breath and turned her tear-stained face towards Stelia. "He knew he was going to die. He knew it. And I knew it, and I couldn't stop him. I couldn't stop it from happening." Tears tracked down her cheeks.

Stelia felt tears well up in her eyes. Clara had lost so much. They all had. "I hate prophecy," she said simply.

"I don't understand why the Lord would send me those dreams, and then make them come true in front of me," Clara said.

"He has a plan for each of us," said Stelia. "I've always been glad not to know the plan he has for me." She smiled slightly, and rubbed Clara's shoulder. "It's a heavy burden you carry, but you must know that He carries it with you. The way His light saved us today; that was a miracle, a God-given miracle given to all of us through His Champion."

"I know," Clara said. Her tears finally slowed. "His light filled me up and healed me." Then she looked down at Adrian again. "So why do I still feel this pain, this . . . almost-doubt? Why is my sword broken?" She held out the hilt to Stelia.

Stelia took it gingerly. When Clara had been ill, she hadn't been able to touch the hilt. Now, it rested in her palm with only a slight warning buzz of warmth in her fingers. "It is still a blade of power," she said, noticing the glow in the jagged edges that protruded from the hilt. She handed it back to Clara. "I'm sure there is a reason."

"I don't understand it, and I don't understand why my mom and my dad, Kryssander and Adrian had to die."

"Everyone has to die to this life to enter the Lord's rest," Stelia said gently. "I know I'm not a mother or a father, but I'm still here." She held out her arms.

Clara grabbed onto her, and leaned into her shoulder. She laughed a tiny laugh. "You're just has hard to hug as my mother," she said, with a tinge of both humor and sadness.

Stelia squeezed her without saying anything for a moment, and then let her go. "Remember, you are loved. You are loved by the Lord, by me, by Master Dantor, Salene, Helena, and many others."

"Master Dantor? He's too gruff to love anyone," Clara said lightly.

Stelia laughed. "Well, he loves me, and he loves all of his students, even if he's tough on them." She let Clara go, and watched as the girl's face brightened slightly.

"I know," Clara said. "I'm glad . . .that . . . well, you know." Her cheeks pinked.

Stelia smiled broadly. "Don't worry; I won't give you any details about falling in love with Dantor."

"That's good," Clara said firmly.

Stelia chuckled a little, and then looked around them at the battlefield. Grimness settled over her. "There is a time for laughter even amidst the tears, but there is also unpleasant work to be done yet."

"What happened to the Drinaii and the Dark Sisters, and . . . .

Kalidess?" Clara asked.

"The Drinaii have fled, the Dark Sisters burned, and Kalidess escaped," Stelia summed up. "I wanted to chase her down, but I fear that she has a head start now. I don't know if she'll return to Skycliff and gather her forces there, or if she slink away into whatever hidey hole she's using these days."

"We'll find her and deal with her," Clara said. She stood up, and fingered the hilt of her sword, turning it to catch the sun's light on the shards of the crystal. "It may not be today, but Kalidess's last day will come." Then nodding to herself, she sheathed the broken blade in her scabbard.

38 A WEEK LATER

Trumpets woke the city of Skycliff, and rang throughout all of the seven districts of Septily. All the people of Septily were gathering to celebrate their victory over the darkness, and the crowning of their new King.

Unable to sleep for a full night, Clara had been up before the light of dawn, praying and thinking over the events of the last few weeks, searching the scriptures and her heart for answers. Hearing the trumpets, she slowly stretched out from her meditative pose, and then stood somewhat stiffly.

A soft knock on her door roused her further from her thoughts, and she simply said, "Come."

Salene paused in the doorway, gazing at her seriously. "You know, if you're going to study all night, you should light a few more lamps." She smiled softly, and then came in, putting her arms around Clara in a gentle hug. "I miss the old us."

"You mean, the two girls who pulled on those silly pranks that you didn't like at the time?" Clara asked, while hugging her back.

"Yes," Salene said, pulling back, and then gesturing at her outfit. "So, what do you think?"

"You look like a noble lady, a girl fit to be betrothed to our King, and yet . . ." Clara took in the full outfit, noticing that the overskirt had slits up the side and underneath, Salene wore leggings, "martial enough to be named our King's protector."

"That's good, I think," Salene said. She frowned a little. "You know, living as an out of favor noble from the Desert province without the honor of the king is nothing like living as a noble accepted by the royal court. I miss being just a sword apprentice."

Clara smiled wryly. "I think it was easier being a sword apprentice looking forward to getting her crystal sword, and not being the Champion with the broken blade." She reached over and picked up her sword belt, and put it on, and then picked up her hilt with its jagged edges reflecting multiple versions of her grim countenance. "I have to fix it somehow," she said.

"Prince William wants you to stay in Skycliff as his advisor," Salene said, reaching out to put her arm on Clara's wrist. "But I want you to do whatever the Lord is calling you to do in your heart."

"Thank you, Salene," Clara said. Then she turned the blade so that it reflected Salene's face. "What do you see?" she asked.

"A broken mirror," Salene said.

"Exactly," Clara said. "I have to heal the blade to heal myself."

"I though the Lord had already-

"Yes, he did, but I feel he wants me to seek Him, to seek the place where this can be fixed," Clara said. "The darkness has been encroaching on the lands of Aramatir for too long."

"So, your mission is beyond Septily?" Salene said.

"I think so," Clara said. She put her left hand over Salene's hand that still rested on her wrist. "I'll miss you," she said, "but I know you have your duty here."

"A duty of dress up," said Salene, pulling away to twirl her skirts.

Clara laughed. "Do you remember when we switched Lady Isabel's makeup with that foot powder?"

"Don't even think about doing that to me!" Salene said, but she chuckled.

"You are nothing like Lady Isabel, so I can't imagine anyone even being tempted," Clara reassured her. "Remember the way she treated Master Dantor?"

"We were defending his honor," Salene said, semi-serious. "I still wonder why she hated him so much."

"There's always things we wonder about it, old stories we don't know," Clara said, thinking about the secretive past of her parents. She wanted to ask Stelia, but no time seemed like the right one.

Salene seemed to sense her change of mood. "What are you wearing for the ceremony?"

"I was sent a Master Swordsman's outfit in white. Can you believe a swordswoman in white?"

"You're the champion," Salene said. "White suits you."

Clara shrugged uncomfortably. "At least it's not a dress."

"True," Salene said. "But this one isn't so bad since I am to be named the Defender. I don't have to wear corsets or hoops or any such nonsense."

Clara nodded. She remembered when she first met Salene in the Desert province. Salene had been wearing the full noble's get up for a child, which included a silly hoop skirt that she couldn't move in. Clara had challenged her to a bout, and Salene had torn off the hoops when she lost. It was so long ago now, and the memories seem to be slipping away to be replaced by these grown up moments.

"I should get dressed for the ceremony," she said.

"That's the official reason I came . . . 'to ensure that the Champion is prepared','" Salene said, putting on an officious manner.

"Aah, Seneschal Bund has been speaking to you," Clara said. She could just imagine the man's face if she didn't dress up. But it wouldn't be worth it, if it hurt her friends, or the Triune Halls. "I'll be quick," she said.

"Good," Salene said, and then she reached out and gave Clara a hug. "I'll see you after all the ceremony."

When Salene left, the room felt empty. Clara sighed, and then started changing into the formal attire of a Sword Master and Champion for the Crown Ceremony.

The white pants and shirt were soft and surprisingly comfortable. Clara enjoyed the feel of them on her skin. Then she put on her armor, piece by piece, and tucked her newly polished helm under her arm. She looked at her travel kit for a moment, and then put the helmet down again. She cleaned off the outside of the pouch with a cleaning cloth, and then attached it to its usual place on her belt. It felt right, but the brown probably stood out.

Clara decided that it didn't matter if it did stand out. She needed the weight against her back to know that she wasn't going to be sucked into court politics. She had a duty to perform for the Lord, and for her country, and it included travel. Finally, with her helmet re-tucked her arm, she left the room without a backward glance.

The hallways were bustling with apprentices, students and Masters all going from one place to another, in last minute preparations. Moving into the Triune Halls barracks seemed like a good idea when she had returned to Skycliff, because her family apartment held too many memories. However, in moments like this, when she had to press herself against the side of the wall to avoid getting trampled on by a group of unruly apprentices running down the hall, she wasn't sure it was a good place for her.

The apprentices were rebuked by their teacher, and they turned to apologize to her. She waved her hand, and they seemed to notice her clothes and her armor for the first time.

"Champion," one of them said, and bowed his head.

The others followed suit, and Clara wished she could leave, but knew that wouldn't be wise. "Please, stop," she said. "Don't bow to me."

"As you wish, Champion," said the first one. He couldn't have been more than a few years younger than her, and although they hadn't had any classes together, it felt very wrong for him to show her that kind of respect.

"My name's Clara," she said, "What's yours?"

He gaped at her for a moment, then said, "um, it's Tristan, Champion."

"Please, Tristan, just call me Clara," she said. "I'm really only a Master because of this," she pointed to the hilt of her sword, "and it's not really much different than being a senior apprentice. I still have a lot to learn."

"All right, um, Clara," he said, still ducking his head a little as if to bow.

"Tell your friends, that I don't stand on formalities," she said.

"Of course she doesn't," said a sneering voice from a few feet away.

Clara turned to see Jazeen, one of her least favorite senior apprentices. Jazeen, who's once lustrous hair had been the envy of most of the other female apprentices, was gaunt and tired looking, and her hair had been shorn short. She had been in hiding under the Halls for the duration of Kalidess's stay in Skycliff, and had nearly starved.

"Jazeen," Clara said, "I'm so glad to see you're out of the infirmary."

"hmmph. A real Champion would have never allowed Kalidess to get a hold of her city."

"You shouldn't speak to her that way, Jazeen," said Tristan.

"It's all right, Tristan," said Clara, "She's only saying things I've thought myself already." She looked into Jazeen's pain-filled eyes until Jazeen dropped her gaze. "We've all lost loved ones, and my regrets are greater than my accomplishments. Somehow, the Lord chose me, and still wants me as His Champion. I seek His guidance and His will alone."

Jazeen mumbled something inaudible, and then brushed past Clara, and kept moving down the crowded hallway.

Tristan moved to stop her, but Clara put her hand out. "Let her go, Tristan."

He glared at Jazeen's retreating back but he nodded. "Champion Clara, your sacrifices and your actions should be honored, even by Jazeen, but for you, I will let her pass."

"Thank you," Clara said. Then she gave him a small salute, and continued on her path, towards the Castle.

As she walked, she noticed that she seemed to be in a bubble of some kind. No one approached her, but they seemed to be talking about her, some smiling and saluting, and some whispering and shaking their heads. All of her friends and her mentors seemed to be absent. Clara tried to hold herself erect and strong, squaring her shoulders and striding out of the Triune Halls and into the courtyard. The bubble held for a few more minutes, until finally, thankfully, a bundle of green ran towards her.

"Clara, Clara," yelled Helena, throwing her arms around Clara's stomach.

"Helena," Clara said, giving her a squeeze.

"I'm in the ceremony today," she said quietly.

"I had heard that," Clara said, thinking of the dull explanation of the ceremony given to her by the seneschal just the day before. "I'm glad that you'll be by my side." She smiled at Helena. "Maybe you could hold my hand," she said.

"I could," said Helena, with a small smile.

39 CEREMONY

Stelia stood near the front of the Triune Hall Courtyard, on the right side of the temporary platform. Dantor stood next to her, looking fine in his ceremonial uniform and armor. The black crystal and his black sleeves stood out in the brightness of all the colors of the Sword Masters around them. Her own burnished amber seemed quiet in the riot of colors, and she felt like a small patch of earth in a bright field of flowers. Not that heavily armed Sword Masters could really be compared to flowers. They looked like varied colored pennants standing strong against the sandstone bricks and the blue sky of the courtyard. She guessed she was more like one of the bricks. She smiled to herself at the thought of being an unmovable stone.

Stelia looked around the whole crowd, scanning and watching at all times for any sign of disturbance or trouble. She didn't expect any, and there hadn't been any sign of such so far, but she wasn't about to let down her guard in a crowd like this. All of Skycliff seemed to be present, stuffed into the courtyard, along Skycliff's walls, and beyond the wide courtyard entrance in throngs that lined the streets.

The noise of chatter rose and fell as people waited for the arrival of their Crown Prince, his Defender, and the Champion.

Finally, the trumpets sounded from the castle, and the crowd quieted. A series of drumbeats boomed, and then boomed again, solidifying into a marching beat. Everyone peered to the edge of the courtyard in anticipation, and Stelia found herself following all the rest for a moment. Then she stopped herself, and started scanning the crowd again.

Next to her, Dantor leaned in closer, and whispered, "Ever a watchful eye, that's one of the things I love about you."

Stelia felt warmth rising to her cheeks and she looked at him for a moment. "Well, one of us needs to keep a look out."

"I am," he said, gazing at her steadily.

"Stop, you're distracting me," she said, smiling in spite of herself. She tore her gaze away from his deep brown eyes, and watched the crowd again. Nothing seemed out of the ordinary, but she knew this would be the perfect time for an assassin to make his or her final preparations.

"We have guards," he said.

"Who are all watching the ceremony," she said.

He sighed, "all right."

The drumbeats were closer now, and finally, the drummer marched into view, leading a full marching band.

Behind them walked Prince William, and King Alexandros, blind and leaning on his son's arm. Behind them came the three highest members of the Triune Halls of Septily, Master Theran of the Sword Hall, Master Jordan of the Shepherd Hall, and Master Gerdun of the Hall of Law. Clara, dressed in a dazzling white shirt and pants under her armor, with her helm tucked under her left arm strode next to Salene who wore a purple tunic with long flowing sides, and loose purple pants under her armor. She carried her helm under her left arm as well, but she looked slightly less martial than Clara. Partly the effect was due to her flowing tunic, and partly due to the fact that she walked the delicacy of a noble sword master, while Clara walked with more of determined rhythm, still graceful but full of deadly purpose.

As the procession reached the courtyard, the crowd there fell completely silent, except for a few murmurs of small children.

The drums beat their rhythm until they reached the steps to the raised platform. Then the drummers lined up at the side of those steps, and stopped drumming.

Prince William looked regal and strong as he led his father up the platform, making sure his father kept his footing. The King looked weak, and worn. The burns from his ordeal had left him bald, but he refused to wear a crown, saying it pained him. The royal dressmakers had done the best they could to hide the burns on his body with a flowing robe of dark blue. Prince William wore a dark purple under his armor. King Alexandros held no staff of office, and if not for the richness of the fabric of his robe, he could have been mistaken for a commoner. When they reached the center of the dais, they stopped, and turned to face the crowd.

The Triune Hall Masters joined them, taking positions to the left of them. Salene and Clara mounted the platform on the right of them. A large space on each side of them was left open, and although Stelia knew what was coming, she was almost drawn into the gasp of the crowd as two griffins swept down from the sky, and landed on the sides of the platform with perfect precision. Helena and Rhodri dismounted Hashani with ease, taking their places next to Clara. Helena slipped her hand into Clara's, and Clara looked down at her and smiled. The crowd sighed a little. Stelia smiled. She knew Clara would never have planned such a moment, but moments like that were the kind that would dispel any of the worst rumors about her broken sword and her possible lack of faith.

The larger griffin held two adults, who both slide dismounted immediately. One of the adults was the Head of the Watch, and the other was an ambassador from Aerland.

From the crowd opposite from Stelia and Dantor, a delegation from Trader's Island and the Isles of Destiny stepped forward. Then it was Stelia and Dantor's turn. They moved forward as one, and Stelia realized that she could no longer scan the crowd unobserved. Her watch would be limited to the people closest to the stage and behind it. She would have to trust the guards with the rest.

Shepherd Jordan stepped forward and held up his hands. "Let us begin today in prayer." He began to pray, with his eyes uplifted to the heavens, and Stelia joined in the prayer with her mind, but kept her eyes open.

"Lord, you have saved us, and made us new, you have led us here today, and we praise you for your goodness and mercy. Help us walk forward in wisdom, and know your will for our people. Amen."

Shepherd Jordan stepped back, and Lawgiver Gerdun stepped forward, opening his hands to the sides in a gesture of goodwill.

"We are gathered here today to begin a new era for Septily under a new King, and a new pledge of service. We ask that you honor this day with your vows, with your hearts, and with your strength." He turned to King Alexandros, and said, "Do you, King Alexandros, wish to hand down your right of kingship?"

King Alexandros bowed his blind face, and said, "My right of Kingship is no longer truly my right, but I do pass it down, into the hands of the Triune Halls, the people of Septily, and my son, Prince William. I pray that he will be a far more honorable and righteous King than I ever was."

The crowd murmured, and then a cry came from the roof of the Triune Halls, "Traitor!" A flaming arrow shot towards the dais, but before it could reach any of its intended recipients, Clara took a step in front of the king and held up her broken blade. Light encased the arrow, and when it dimmed the arrow felt burnt to the ground.

Guards ran to the roof, and a scuffle ensued, and then stopped. One of the guards raised his voice over the consternation of the crowd. "All clear."

"Thank you, Champion," said Gerdun.

Clara bowed her head slightly and sheathed the broken blade.

The King looked very upset, and knelt down on the platform, tears streaming down his cheeks. William reached down and helped his father up. The King leaned on him for support, and looked down at the platform with his shoulders slumped.

Lawgiver Gerdun returned to the ceremony, gesturing to Rhodri who stood on the outside by the lady griffin. Rhodri stepped forward with a circlet resting on a small pillow. Gerdun took the crown reverently, and held it up towards the crowd. "It is my honor, and the honor of the Triune Halls, to bestow this crown on the rightful, and sanctioned heir for the throne, Prince William." He turned to facc William. "Do you, Prince William accept this crown and the responsibilities that go with it?"

"I do," said Prince William.

"Do you pledge your life to serve the people of Septily?

"I pledge my life to serve the Lord and the people of Septily."

"Will you place the wisdom of the Lord, the guidance of the Triune Halls, and the well-being of your people above your own wishes?"

"I will," said William. "The Lord rules, the Triune Council guides, and the well-being of my people is above my personal wishes."

"You may kneel, to show your service to all," said Gerdun.

Prince William gently let go of his father, and then stepped forward and knelt down by Gerdun. He bowed his head.

Stelia wondered if this was normal for the crowning ceremony of Septily, and she looked for a moment at Dantor.

As if reading her mind, he smiled slightly and shook his head.

Gerdun placed the crown on William's head, and called the other Triune leaders forward. The three men placed their hands on William's head, and then Shepherd Jordan led them in prayer.

"May the Lord give us wisdom and guidance, may we do his will above ours, may Prince William honor the Lord and all his vows, and may we help him in this endeavor. Amen."

The crowd murmured their response, and then Prince – no, King William rose to his feet. His face looked somber, and he gazed steadily out at the crowd.

"I now present to you, Septily, your new King," said Gerdun.

The whole crowd erupted in cheers, whistles and applause. Stelia added her own voice to the throng, but also kept an eye on the people around them. Everyone looked genuinely joyous. Smiles and bright faces ringed the stage.

King William held up his hands, in a gesture for quiet, and the crowd subdued slowly, still leaning forward eagerly for his words. His face looked bright but solemn. "Countrymen and Friends, Hall Masters and Allies, I thank you for this honor. I pray that I will stay true to the Lord and worthy of your trust each and every day." He paused, and then held out his hands towards his father. "My father, Alexandros has shared with me his regret for his actions, and as you know, the sword of Septily's Kings was tarnished in the war with the Dark Sisterhood and the Drinaii. We hope someday, to find a new blade for the Kings of Septily. For now, the only sword I have to offer you is this plain sword," he unsheathed his weapon of plain steel and held it up for everyone to see. Then he sheathed it again. "However, I know that the Lord has plans for our land, for my rule, and I know that we have many strong sword masters as our defenders."

A small cheer arose from the ranks of the Sword Hall.

King William smiled. "We also have wise Shepherds, and well-versed Law-givers to keep us on the right path."

The two other groups now cheered.

"We have a strong nation of people who are committed to one another, and to our Lord. We have allies who help us in times of trouble, and as King I pledge to keep our alliances strong and to seek out new alliances."

Applause greeted his words, and Stelia noted that the ambassadors smiled and looked pleased, included the griffins, who cocked their heads slightly.

"One of the alliances I will start today is one that will affect me personally," King William paused and turned slowly towards Salene. "I have asked Lord Gray to resume his post as Governor of the Desert Province, and I have asked for his daughter's hand in marriage." He reached out his hand, and Salene took it and walked forward.

"May I present to you, Lady Salene Gray, my betrothed and First Defender," King William said.

Salene curtseyed, and then stood next to King William, facing the crowd. She smiled quietly at him and then at the gathering.

An appreciative oohing went through the crowd, and then applause. Salene blushed slightly, and looked over at William, who shared her look for a moment before turning to address the crowd again.

His face took on a solemn demeanor again, no longer smiling. "As you know, our country faced destruction under the Dark Sisterhood and the Drinaii. Our lives and our land were spared only through the intervention of the Lord, and His hand on one particular person, his Champion." William paused and looked at Clara.

Clara looked at him, and then the crowd, and then down at Helena. She let go of the little girl's hand, and took her place on William's other side.

"Champion Clara lost her family in the darkness that covered our people, and her sword, the sword of Champions was broken by poison."

Clara bit her lip, looking strained and fingering the hilt of her sword.

"But as you have seen today, the light of the Lord still shines through her. She was broken, but yet she regained her faith. Her life and her sacrifice are a lesson to us all. Even in the darkest moments, we can trust that the Lord will save us if we trust in Him."

The crowd cheered loudly, and then again.

King William put his free hand on Clara's shoulder. "Champion Clara symbolizes the faith we must have to push back the darkness in Septily and beyond. Our allies need us, and those who were once our allies need us even more. As our country recovers from the recent battle, the Triune Council will seek out our allies, and we will do all that we can to force the darkness off Brythan Continent and if possible, our world of Aramatir."

More cheering ensued, and then, the drummers took up their beat again. The procession reversed down the platform, and started back towards the King's castle.

Stelia and Dantor were swept up into the procession, and flanked

Clara who now walked alone. Stelia could see from the line of Clara's shoulders that the girl was upset so she walked forward so that she was even with her. Dantor joined them on Clara's other side.

40 MEMORIAL

The crowd in the Triune Halls courtyard had been boisterous and full of cheer. As the procession walked from the courtyard to the Memorial Grounds, the crowd quieted and became somber. Despite that, Clara knew that she was being watched. She didn't like being on display, and wasn't sure how Salene could handle the idea of a life like this one stretching ahead of her.

She felt thankful for Stelia and Master Dantor's presence on each side of her, protecting her from the crowd as much as they could.

The walk to the Memorial Grounds became a blur as Clara focused inward on memories of her mom and dad, of the life they had lived.

It startled her when the processional line widened out and fell into a line by a row of graves. A four mile walk from the city's center to the Memorial Grounds seemed to have passed in a moment. She looked over at Master Dantor, and saw that he looked at the graves, his lips pressed into a hard line. On the other side of her, Stelia looked haunted, her face drawn and tight.

Clara stared at the graves now, still covered in fresh dirt, and the stone memorials for those whose bodies could either not be recovered or whose traditions demanded other types of rituals than burial. Clara had been shocked to learn that the Aerlandians burned their dead on high platforms. It seemed wrong, and yet, very little in the scriptures covered the practices of mourning the dead. To the right of the royal family's burial crypt, the Allied Memorial stood as a long white wall. On one end, fresh carvings had been made for Adrian and Kryssander, as well as many other allies who had fallen on the battle field.

Shepherd Jordan now stood in front of the group and addressed them. "We come to remember, to honor those who have sacrificed their lives for our freedom and for the Lord's glory. Despite our grief, we know that they are in a new place, a place where no more tears are shed, no more pains are felt. They are with the Lord in his heavenly dwelling place, and we are left with new horizons before us, seemingly empty with our loss. But the Lord has plans for us."

Clara listened to his words, and then she drifted again into memories, numbly aware of the continued proceedings around her. As the others left, she stayed on with just a few around her. Finally, only Stelia stood by her side.

"Stay for a while in Skycliff, Clara," she said gently.

"What?" Clara felt shaken from her grief for a moment.

"I see your kit on your belt, and I know you want to pursue the destiny set before you, but I ask you to stay, just for a little while. We have, I think, something to talk about before you go."

Clara swallowed. "About my mother?"

"Yes," Stelia said gently. She put her hand on Clara's shoulder for a moment. "And other things." She looked over the Memorial Grounds, and then back to Clara. "But not now."

Clara nodded. She didn't think she could handle anything else right now, with the lump in her chest, and the heaviness of her heart.

"I'll see you back in the Triune Halls," Stelia said, and then she squeezed Clara's shoulder and left, following some of the other late stragglers down the main path towards the road.

Clara walked to the Allied Memorial wall, and went to the inscription for Adrian and Kryssander. "Adrian and Kryssander of Aerland," were the words printed on the stone. It was too simple, and didn't say enough. However, the Aerlandian ambassadors seemed to approve since their people did not keep such things as gravestones.

Clara put her hand on the cool stone, and thought of both of them, flashes of their one day together when she had been awake. It seemed impossible that those hours held such significance and burned so brightly, and yet they did. Tears rolled down her cheeks, and she let them for the first time.

Finally, she looked up again. The calm light gray clouds overhead seemed to echo her mood, not bright but not grim. She simply felt empty. The loss of her mom and dad, of Adrian and Kryssander had emptied her out. The Lord's presence felt certain and comforting, but yet, she knew that there was more to life.

She was waiting. Waiting for life to start again, or waiting for the next hardship, she wasn't sure, but she knew that she was in between things. She stood, and looked over the graveyard. So many fresh graves, and yet so many that were unburied. She walked to the marker that stood for her parents. Intertwined roses were carved into the cross, with their names on each arm, and a symbol for each of their offices. She touched the cool stone, and ran her fingers over the etched lines. The rough stone felt strong under her fingers. Kneeling there, she spent time remembering each of them, their voices, their faces, their laughter, and their love. She had been blessed to have such parents, and she knew she would mourn them again and again. Missing their presence in her life was just part of the daily pattern she followed now.

Finally, she stood up, and looked around her. Gravestones and memorial sites stretched to the far reaches of the field. A new field would have to be purchased in the next year; a grim reminder of the losses that Septily had suffered under Kalidess's short reign.

Her gaze turned to the road from the Memorial Grounds which shortly connected the main roads. Walking away from the graves, she went to the main road. She looked left, at the city of Skycliff, rising with the land above the ocean, ending at the tip with the Triune Halls. Flags snapped in the wind, and people's voices created a joyful hubbub of noise. To the right, the quiet road wound through fields and forests, and then around a hill. She took a step in that direction and then she dropped her hand to the hilt of her sword.

It wasn't time yet, but soon, it would be.

ACKNOWLEDGMENTS

Every book may stem from the imagination of one writer, but the roots that give the story strength branch out in many directions, deep in the rich soil of encouragement. The rain that falls on the story plant give it life, and the wind that threatens to break it, just gives it strength. This little section is for all of you who have given me rich encouragement and life-giving guidance, but it's also for the ones who have been the wind, that unknowingly strengthened my resolve.

My mom and dad gave me the freedom to daydream, and read my early drafts, giving me encouragement. My husband John believed in me every step of the way, and became my formatter at the last minute. My daughter Anna encouraged me to turn a short story into a novel. My daughter Trisha created the first cover for this book, and helped me edit with a discerning eye for detail. Thank you dear family!

My critique partner, Nickie Anderson, became an invaluable ally in editing my book. She gave me just the right feedback to get my characters more real on the page, and because of her well-worded help, I finally changed my villainess's name to something pronounceable. Thank you Nickie!

My niece, Stephanie Glover, jumped at the chance to become my cover artist. She brought my ideas to life with her artwork, and helped me visualize my characters in fuller detail. Thank you Stephanie!

There are countless others who have encouraged me along this writing journey, and I know I won't be able to name them all, but for now I thank: Susan Wilborn, Grace Nichols, Allison, Jamie Ayres, Alex J. Cavanaugh, Dianne L. Gardner, Laurel Garver, Laura Josephsen, Karen Lange, Livia Peterson, Susan Kaye Quinn, Cherie Reich, Carol Riggs, Tara Tyler, for all the IWSG writers, and all my other blog buddies who have given me feedback, and most importantly, encouragement!!

ABOUT THE AUTHOR

Tyrean Martinson lives and writes in the Northwest, encouraged by her loving husband and daughters, and reminded to exercise by her dogs and cat. Champion in the Darkness is her first book, but she has had short stories and poetry previously published online at e-zines and in print in anthologies. She can be found online at Tyrean's Writing Spot: http://tyreanswritingspot.blogspot.com/